T0248156

RUDE BUAY

... The Untouchable

An Original Story
By
National Bestselling Author
John A. Andrews
Creator Of:
The Rude Buay Series

Published in the U.S.A. by
Books That Will Enhance Your Life™
www.booksthatwillenhanceyourlife.com

A L I - Andrews Leadership International
Entertainment Division®
Jon Jef Jam Entertainment®
www.AndrewsLeadershipInternational.com

Cover Design: John A. Andrews
Cover Graphic Designer: A L I
Edited by: Prof. Harminder Kaur
ISBN: 9780983845775

Other Titles
By:
John A. Andrews

How I Raised Myself from Failure to Success in Hollywood
Dare To Make A Difference – Success 101 For Teens
When The Dust Settles - A True Hollywood Story
Total Commitment - The Mindset of Champions
The 5 Steps to Changing Your Life
How I Wrote 8 Books In One Year
Whose Woman Was She?
The FIVE "Ps" For Teens
Cross Atlantic Fiasco
&
Quotes Unlimited

TABLE OF CONTENTS

"I firmly believe that any man's finest hour,
the greatest fulfillment of all that he holds
dear, is the moment when he has worked his
heart out in a good cause and lies exhausted
on the field of battle - victorious"

-       VINCE LOMBARDI

http://thinkexist.com/quotation/i_firmly_believe_that_any_ma
n-s_finest_hour-the/173395.html

The
RUDE BUAY
Series

Vol. II

The Ride Continues ...

THE HOSPITAL LOBBY IS CROWDED with Jamaican police officers. Banks is pushed around in a wheel chair with his left arm in a sling. The Police commissioner, Mildred and Rude Buay admire compassionately. Rude Buay walks up to Banks, and hands over to him an attaché' case. Banks opens it. He smiles upon seeing the stacks of crisp C notes. He closes the attaché' case then gives Rude Buay thumbs up and departs. Agent Hudson walks out from the discharge room, accompanied by Tamara. Rude Buay greets agent Hudson smilingly. They turn to leave. Richard Baptiste steps into their space, and utters –

"Thanks Rude Buay."

"My pleasure,"

Says Rude Buay.

Tamara rushes past the commissioner, right into Rude Buay's space. Their eyes become locked momentarily. Mildred moves closer towards Rude Buay, scrutinizing her.

"Rude Buay, you forgot something," says Tamara.

"My vest!"

She flies into his arms. Mildred eyes them enviously.

1

A dense mixture of blackened and gray clouds open up to sparse streaks of lightning, followed by severe intermittent thunder storms. Torrent rain showers burst out of those sporadic illuminated clouds as a follow up to the rumbling fiery interlude. Meanwhile, trees sway noisily, splitting into halves at their trunks, sending splinters of timber flying in the distance. Additionally, the downed power lines, and the uprooting of multiple plants, seem to indicate that whatever is about to happen in Port Antonio, Jamaica, on this mid Friday afternoon is more than just a severe rain storm.

It could possibly equal or top the destruction of Port Royal back in the 1692.

"Could this be *Déjà Vu* or what some may call voodoo? These inclement weather conditions are not felt elsewhere, not even in another parish on the Island. Weather conditions have not been this severe since Mount St. Helens blew its top sending trees downstream or since the destruction of Port Royal in 1692." One enthusiastic yet subdued radio announcer with a sophisticated British twang, candidly remarks. Patrons at a Port Antonio restaurant, not only hear and watch the news but feel the earth tremble continually and intermittently for several minutes, while the sea roars like a hungry lion, adding to mother nature's audio effects.

Meanwhile, at sea high magnitude waves boisterously crash against protruding rocks and the battered shoreline.

Small crafts sway as they get tossed back and forth by the wind. Some crafts under duress, even sever the ropes which ties them to the small wooden dock. HUGE wave forms in succession. Sand, gravel and the last waves' deposits are removed from the shore, and then viciously REDEPOSITED on the debris saturated beach.

Nervously and securely docking his boat, a frazzled American Sailor senses futility as the dock which held his twenty-two foot *Casper* collapses. The raging storms eventually and hastily send his small vessel and others alike into the now tsunami like waves of the ocean.

While watching his boat tossed away in the current, the Sailor; like the enthusiastic famous crocodile catcher from Australia; fights the treacherous waves as he swims back to shore in an investigative pursuit of the human carcass which just washed ashore.

The sailor rushes to the beach as the waves draw back to support the next oncoming surge. With his hand covering his nostrils, he runs over to the mostly decomposed body in investigative pursuit. The body is motionless. The sailor gets a close up of the man's corpse. In the corpse's left hand tightly clenched, he bears the leg portion of a multicolored wet suit. The Sailor, not only drenched, but remains startled by the dramatic unfolding toxic scene.

In the subsequent moments, the rain recedes as a long extended rainbow decorates the flustered, angry, still overcast cloudy sky.

The Sailor embraces the opportunity to call 911 using his rubber cased protected cell phone, retrieved from his seat pocket.

He enthusiastically yells into the device, drowning out the sound of the waves. His voice echoes in the distance.

"...My boat *Casper* is gone! All the boats have been pulled out to the ocean. A man, a dead man! I swear, so dead he filthy rots. The corpse sports a dragon tattoo behind his almost decomposed right ear lobe. He looks multi-ethnic-mixed, could be of Hispanic decent, in his mid-forties. He has a missing index finger and expensive gold rings on the four fingers of his right hand. In his tightly clenched left fist is a wetsuit. His grasp on it is so tight not even the rough seas had a chance to dislodge this object from his lifeless hands. What an ... eclipse!"

MOMENTS LATER, FLASHING LIGHTS accompany the coroners' vehicle, with Jamaican Police vehicles in tow. They race to the scene. The medics quickly place the "washed ashore human body" in a body bag and haul it away aboard the coroner's transport.

2

In the interim, retrospectively over a thousand miles away, it is a beautiful sunny day in St. Georges, Grenada. The GRENADA TV weatherman takes his reporting to another level by boasting the clarity of the sky and the warm water beaches in and around the capital city. This much smaller Island to the south is nestled between St. Vincent and the Grenadines a group of 32 Islands, neighboring Trinidad and Tobago, two Islands in the Greater Antilles.

In the meantime, the brisk wind coupled with the heat, extracts the spicy aroma from a variety of produce. In particular, those transported to the market by late afternoon vendors in pickup trucks.

The savory spicy fragrances saturate the air. Ships, arriving and departing toot their horns as they signal their mix with the sailing traffic.

A few blocks away, several people including priest and other dignitaries congregate. ALBERTO GOMEZ, drug Czar, and leader of the Dragon Drug Cartel emerges. The man who was once assumed dead after a most recent *high-seas* shoot out with DEA agent Rude Buay, back in Jamaica.

Alberto is dressed in an expensive business suit and dark glasses. He is mid to late 30s, and Colombian descent. The Drug Czar is poised with a pair of scissors in hand.

"Ladies and gentlemen today we celebrate a new landmark in the history of the Caribbean. This library stands as a cornerstone to the men and women...of tomorrow. What good is a man if he ducks ... his own education? Worthless! Your children's future has never looked brighter."

Alberto addresses,

He cuts the ribbon to the sound of a standing ovation, and applause, accompanied by a brief interlude of steel band music.

The librarian, a Caucasian woman in her early 50s, wearing spectacles, and proudly displaying her name tag: VERONICA TOWNSVILLE, saunters across and proudly shakes Alberto's hand.

DAVID LEE, Entrepreneur and Asian Drug Czar, wearing an expensive suit and dark sunglasses, AMBLES through the crowd.

David hands Alberto a slip of paper.

Alberto reads the handwritten note and accompanies David back to his car.

They embark.

The car driven by Lee takes off SPEEDILY.

3

Just a few blocks AWAY, at the Grenada Medical
School, the car pulls up.
Alberto Gomez steps out of the car.
The car continues.
With a clipboard and pen in hand, Alberto urges the
students charismatically
"Sign up for educational funding! The future of your
country, rest in your hands, not in your government."
It's not long before he attracts an enormous crowd.
Amongst the gathering, several enthusiasts line up
and eagerly sign up in response to his plea.

In the crowd AMANDA KINGSLEY stands out. Amanda is a tall African American woman, in her late 30s. Amanda softens her stern demeanor as she looks out at the growing line of candidates, all waiting to benefit from her boss' financial aid program. Alberto makes eye contact with her. She evolves and with sophistication handles the dense crowd.

After satisfying the many would be students Alberto and Amanda depart.

Smiles from that soon to be medical fraternity sweeten the two organizers goodbye.

Alberto and Amanda board a waiting taxi.

A black limousine pulls up moments after the taxi drives off.

Agent Randy Bascombe, nicknamed *RUDE BUAY* - aka "Rude Boy" is of Jamaican decent. He exits the car from the rear seat on the driver's side. He's, in his early forties, adorned with a scorpion tattooed on his bald head, with its fangs upstaging his forehead, and tail extending towards his right earlobe. Dressed in street clothes, he steps out.

The agent is unaware that Alberto Gomez and his team have left the building. So he waits in anticipation of Alberto's exit from the medical compound. Alberto is a no show.

To Rude Buay, from the way things look on the outside, everything indicates it's a normal day at any school. Even so, he enters the compound.

A Guard meets and greets him.

"Are you looking for someone?"

The guard asks.

"Where is your restroom?"

Rude Buay inquires.

The guard accommodates nonchalantly.

Rude Buay visits the facility, noticing nothing rather unusual he departs and re-boards the waiting limousine. The limo waits. Rude Buay dials DEA headquarters in Miami.

MICHAEL ORTIZ, in his early 50s replacing the snuffed out Jose Mendez Rude Buay's former boss picks up the buzzing phone.

"This is Rude Buay,"

"How are things in Grenada?"

"Nothing to report on Alberto's whereabouts just yet,"

Rude Buay responds.

"Well we need you back in Miami... seeing that the dead man has not showed up yet."

Ortiz says sarcastically.

Feeling like the last statement is seasoned salt in his wound,

"Why? What is going on in Miami?"

Rude Buay asks double questioningly,

"We can always use a good DEA in Miami. One who can afford to let sleeping dogs lie."

Rude Buay ponders, and ends the call. The Limo makes a hard U-Turn and later arrives outside the airport.

Rude Buay hurries inside the terminal where he boards a plane bound for Miami.

4

One day later. Outside the dock in Montego Bay, a taxi pulls up with two women seated on the rear seat. Alberto saunters from one parked taxi to one with the occupants. He boards on the front passenger seat. On the rear seat, seated is his wife DENISE GOMEZ and SHELLY HALL. Denise is an Asian, trophy woman, in her late twenties. Her engagement ring, touching her wedding band, is to be greatly desired by any woman. The blinding rock speaks for itself. Additionally, Denise's new hairstyle gives her a much sophisticated younger look. Alberto is happy to see her alive and vice versa.

SHELLY HALL, on the other hand is Caucasian, tall and feisty, WWE type. Shelly is in her 30s, wearing a red bandana which color schemes with the healing bruises on her face. Both women are armed with semi-automatics.

Night falls. The taxi pulls up outside the Blue Lagoon Hotel. Alberto and Denise exit the taxi and enter the hotel. Shelly continues the ride to MO BAY airport.

Inside the hotel room, Alberto's newly acquired outfits are still lying on the bed. Among them are nicely tailored suits, and a wetsuit. He goes to the bathroom and discards the upper portion of another wetsuit in the trash and passionately reacquaints himself with Denise.

Alberto's cell phone rings. He answers it.

"*Don Señor* Alberto, the shipment is ready to be picked up, *pronto*,"

The voice of SALVADOR, his Colombian counterpart assures.

Sal, as he is better known, is a Colombian, in his late 30s, and stationed in Bogota. He is basically overseeing the day to day operations of cutting and shipping cocaine to Miami, The Caribbean and Asia. His inaccurate cutting was responsible for the glitch in the lethal Dragon X which caused the death of many Jamaican kids a few months prior.

Salvador hangs up the cellular phone and drives off in his beat up white pickup truck.

"*Gracias,*"

Alberto says.

Alberto dials another number,

Shelly Hall rushing out of the shower with a towel wrapped around her picks up the phone from her hotel room.

"I need you on the plane in the morning heading to Miami. I need a clean job, no flaws."

Alberto demands.

"I'm on it!"

Shelly responds.

5

Later that evening, a private airplane touches down at Dade County Airport in Miami and parks at a hangar. Shelly deplanes, under disguise and dressed to the nines. Shelly's demeanor says she is anxious being back in Miami.

A RASTAFARIAN, wearing a green, yellow and black tam, the colors of Jamaica, with his dreadlocks hairstyle almost touching his butt, greets Shelly. The Rastafarian, hands over a set of keys and an envelope. Shelly opens the envelope. She pulls out the white sheet of paper, on it are written instructions. She

RUDE BUAY VOL. II

reads the note and departs inside the airport terminal en-route to the parking lot. Shelly presses the remote, a black on black Jaguar answers. She hurries to it, gets in and drives away. This automobile is quite her style.

ON THE FOLLOWING MORNING, the sun, after many failed attempts shines some tiny rays of sunlight on the Dade County Prison. This enormous structure nestled in the suburban area of Miami, Florida is a landmark to many. It is public knowledge that the walls are over twenty-five feet below the ground as they are above the ground. They boast a diameter of over three feet in thickness. Built over a hundred years ago, no one has ever escaped those walls. This penitentiary has housed many non celebs as well as big names celebrities.

A midnight blue van pulls out from the facility's underground parking area. It exits the compound and merges with the steady flow of morning traffic. Inside three guards: the driver RAYMOND PEREZ of Cuban decent. Raymond is armed to the max. In the rear: TONY CLINTON Caucasian and DARRELL WEEKS of African American decent. Both men are also armed to the hilt.

Darrell Weeks looks across at his co-worker who has a gun pointed at the prisoner en-route to Miami's maximum security prison. Their man is JOHNNY, alias *"Too Bad."*

23

Johnny is Jamaican of African American decent, who was recently captured in Jamaica and extradited to the America by the U.S. Government. It was claimed that Johnny was one of the most notorious Drug Lords to ever operate on the Island of Jamaica outside of ALBERTO GOMEZ leader of the Dragon Drug Cartel. Johnny ruled Tivoli Gardens. Looking across at Clinton, Johnny remains stone faced while shackled hands and feet.

The Miami Prison Official blue vehicle approaches the Miami Bay Bridge as traffic begins to thin out. A black Jaguar tailing it for more than half a mile speeds up from behind and passes the moving van, slicing its way directly in front of it to avoid a head on collision with an oncoming tractor trailer. The two guards in the back of the prison transport are discombobulated as they grab on to the vehicle's seat for support.

Johnny is shaken up. Even so, he remains poised and stoned faced.

"That is a sick …! Where the heck did she get her driving instructions?"

Raymond the driver mutters.

"She must have bought it in South Beach."

Responds Darrell Weeks.

The correction officers share a jovial laugh in regards to the South Beach allusion.

"BTW, did any of you watch that repo show about South Beach?

Clinton states in gesture.

There is silence as no one seems to get what he is talking about.

He answers his own question by saying,

"It's sick."

Moments later, along the mid-point portion of the bridge, the Jaguar comes to a complete stop.

Before the van could complete its unavoidable rear end collision with the Jaguar, the driver of this chic, luxurious vehicle, Shelly Hall, opens the door. Shelly jumps out of the car and over the bridge, plunging into frigid body of water.

The airbag in the prison vehicle malfunctions. The no seatbelt wearing Perez sails through the front windscreen and out onto the bridge's roadway, head first. Perez's weapons and most of his warden accessories disperse as he crashes hard onto the metal and concrete pavement. He tries to get up but is unable to make it solo. So he falls unconscious back to the ground.

Flustered and in a state of panic Tony Clinton jumps out to assist Perez.

Johnny seizes the opportunity and with full force he "head butts" Darrell Weeks.

The severe blow and impact causes Weeks' head to crash hard against the longitudinal interior of the van. Knocked out, Weeks collapses onto the floor.

Johnny, still chained hand and legs, sits on top of Weeks, now in the fetal position. Johnny seizes the opportunity and searches through the Warden's pockets and retrieves the keys which he uses to set himself free.

Prowling, Johnny darts outside and finishes off Raymond Perez and Tony Clinton, one round of bullets per officer.

Johnny, speedily returns to the van, discharges one round of bullets inside Weeks' mouth finishing him off.

Before making his escape, Johnny pulls out a plastic bag of weed from inside his underwear. It is a large *Ziploc* bag.

He empties the contents on the driver's seat. One whiff of that deposit is enough to get one high and sustain it for hours.

Johnny secures his gun inside the bag, seals the bag, and slides the package inside his waist. He plunges into the frigid water of Miami Bay.

Traffic is at an all-time stand still as the bridge is only now accessible by foot traffic.

The early arrivers seem to want to dive in after Johnny, but they dare carrying out such a feat from so high an altitude and pursuing an armed criminal.

Rescue teams finally press their way through, they plunge into the deep with blood hound dogs. News reporters converge onto the scene. Rescue teams come up empty, as neither Shelly nor Johnny are recovered from the Bay.

HOURS LATER, AND MILES AWAY from the scene, a 75 feet long submarine, made of fiberglass and wood, surfaces and picks up Shelly and Johnny *Too Bad*.

6

ack in Jamaica, a Caucasian woman named
BEVERLY HASTINGS, adorned with a lengthy
dread locks hairstyle, almost touching her butt
is bottle feeding her toddler, Andrew. Beverly is in
her mid-thirties, and at a younger age looked like she
could have been a runway model if she wanted to.
She aborts feeding the five month old Andrew.

Before she could adequately burp Andrew, her three
year old daughter Leticia, once seen sucking the
residue from her bottle falls off the high chair and
onto the floor below.

Beverly puts the toddler in his crib and rushes to her daughter Leticia's aid. Three other kids, two boys and one girl, all under the ages of five rush out of the bedroom to the scene.

Beverly picks up Leticia who is now limp, and in a daze. Leticia's vital signs are almost nil save only for little visual movement in her upper torso.

Beverly tries comforting the little girl in her arms. Finally, Leticia collapses with the climax of one last breath while lying in her mother's arms.

Beverly is not only flustered but mortified. She desperately tries CPR. That doesn't revive her three year old Leticia.

Beverly screams out. So do the other kids, except for baby Andrew who lies innocently in his crib playing with his hanging toys.

Beverly calls 911 and thereafter huddles with three of her kids. They are all sobbing, engulfed in tears.

Moments later, the Medics arrive.

Inquiring Neighbors also show up. The Medics enter the house and return with Leticia on a Gurney. Leticia is rushed away aboard the Medical vehicle.

THE FOLLOWING MORNING, two middle aged women from Child protective Services arrive at Beverly's door. They are officially escorted by Jamaican Police in a squad car. One of the women carrying a clip board knocks on the door.

Beverly answers. The police officers introduce themselves as Officers Bailey and Carter.

Bailey addresses her,

"Miss Hastings, my name is officer Bailey with the Jamaica Police Department and this is Officer Carter. Based on autopsy results it was determined that your daughter Leticia died as a result of a drug overdose. We have been authorized to assist in the removal of four kids: Andrew, Michael, Max and Sherunda Hastings from your custody; pending an investigation."

The officers round up the kids and carry them through the door.

Beverly sheds tears as she witnesses her kids escorted inside the Child Protective Services vehicle.

The officers return to the house. Bailey once again addresses,

"Miss Hastings, I am afraid that we are going to have to take you down to the station for further questioning."

They escort Beverly outside. The two Jamaican police officers shove Beverly inside the rear seat of the squad car. The car departs.

A FEW DAYS LATER, Beverly returns to the house but the kids doesn't. Maintaining her innocence; Beverly in her mind's eye knew that she was framed and just couldn't understand why and by whom.

Even so, she is determined to solve this gruesome mystery.

Beverly sits on the side of the bed smoking Hookah. It poses an enormous challenge for Beverly to recall everything relating to her five orphaned kids, mainly in those moments prior to the mishap. So she decided to calculatingly retrace her steps.

In her mind she relived the entire meal preparation process for little Leticia. Starting with the washing and sterilizing of the feeding bottle to the putting of the eight ounce bottle of milk in Leticia's hand.

Beverly's intuition leads her to the milk can container from which she scooped the milk to make Leticia's meal. Upon opening the can she recalled sensing nothing abnormal. Yet, for some reason she cannot-leave the milk can alone. She read up on the contents, preparing instructions, and even where it was packaged.

Beverly frustratingly turns the can upside down emptying all the powdered milk onto the kitchen table. To her surprise, there is a plastic *Ziploc* bag on the top of the milk pile. The size of the bag averaged at least one eight of a kilo of white substance. While removing it, the powdered contents continuously seep out and onto the heap. Using her pinky finger Beverly takes a taste test. The sordid look on her face indicates that inside the milk container there wasn't all milk. Saddened, her loud scream alert the neighbors.

Some neighbors abandoning their chores in an investigative pursuit. Some of them show up bare-footed.

One woman in particular, shows up wearing her bath robe along with a pair of house slippers. Another woman arrives with one half of her hair styled and the other half still in rollers.

In tears Miss Hastings immediately called 911. Minutes later, her house is now not only filled with visitors but the same two police officers who orchestrated her arrest. They show up. The officers trying to mask their apology confiscate the contaminated combination of milk and cocaine.

They put the can inside the trunk of the squad car and drives off.

7

A light blue sedan pulls up outside the Miami Drug Enforcement office. Before the driver agent Rude Buay, could slam the car door shut, the car built in agent's radio transits.

The voice states, "Requesting DEA presence at Milky Way Warehouse, at the corner of Providence and Dixie Highway. Rude Buay gets back inside his car. Making a swift U-Turn his sedan merges, tires squealing, with the intercepting traffic.

Rude Buay speedily pulls up in-front the warehouse. He jumps out armed but with caution. He notices a man's body, bloodied laying in the gutter. The man's face though bloodied looks familiar.

Rude Buay goes to his car and retrieves a pair of gloves. He rolls the man over for a close up look. Rude Buay shakes his head. He knows him. Rude Buay releases him.

The victim's badge falls out of his jacket pocket along with a Polaroid picture.

Rude Buay confiscates the two pieces of evidence along with the victim's wallet. He puts them in a plastic bag, and lodges the bag inside the car trunk. Rude Buay notices the agent's car across the street. He investigates the agent's car for additional evidence. Moments later, Paramedics arrive and remove the body from the scene. Medics place the body inside a body bag. Miami Police Officers intervene and yellow tape off the area.

Prior to the dispatch call and agent Rude Buay being dispatched to the scene. The victim, undercover agent MARK JONES showed up outside the Milky Way Warehouse and purchased two kilos of cocaine from Shelly Hall.

After the deal was made, FRANKIE O'NEAL, a Colombian in his early 40s, pulled up in a black limousine to fetch her and Johnny. *One Arm Frankie-* as he is nicknamed decked out in a suit and tie, wearing an artificial left arm with a stub and a clip at the end of it is all business.

Shelly and Johnny board the black limo, while the undercover agent walks towards his vehicle. Johnny seated on the limo's front seat rolls the window down, and blows the man's brains out with the stolen warden's gun.

Shelly getting inside the rear of the limo asked,

"Why did you shoot him?"

Johnny responded,

"Just another PIG, who, deserved to die. Every pig ought to be dead; they get in the way of business."

Johnny retrieved the narcotics from the undercover agent and threw it back inside on the rear seat of the limo.

Frankie drove away taking the back roads and side streets, heading towards the Manor on top of the hill.

Back at DEA headquarters, agent Rude Buay tries to glean more detailed information about the Polaroid photo recovered at the crime scene. So he searches the web for all the elite homes in Dade County. He comes up empty. Flustered, he goes to the office next door. No one is there except for a box of Crispy cream doughnuts. He indulges.

Rude Buays' new partner MILES TATE, a Caucasian in his early 30s, whose youthful demeanor says I am really a rookie. He walks in with a soda in hand. In his other hand he is carrying a copy of the chronicle

Rude Buay ... The Unstoppable along with a yellow highlighter.

Tate looking at Rude Buay states,

"I thought you didn't like chocolate,"

Rude Buay replies,

"It looked so good, I couldn't resist."

Rude Buay continues,

"First day on the job, you seem to study people's preference a lot. Plus only overzealous students read with a dual-colored - high-lighter."

Tate responds,

"I was in the Green room and noticed that only chocolate donuts were left in the box. So I assumed you..."

Rude Buay looking at the book in Tate's hand for a second time remarks,

"Reading, killing time or studying?"

Tate replies,

"Digesting and assimilating."

"Have you ever seen this house before, Miles?'

Rude Buay asks pointing to the Polaroid.

Tate responds,

"Never. No sir."

"Who owns this ...?"

Rude Buay questions,

"Your guess is as good as mine, and as well as Mark Jones'."

Tate replies.

"Look it up see what you find."
Rude Buay finishes the doughnut. He picks up the
Polaroid and exits from Green Room.
Tate yells,
"Do you need me for backup?"
Rude Buay responds,
"I got this. Call me if you find something."
Rude Buay hits the streets in his sedan. The car tires
burn rubber upon take off.

8

Rude Buay pulls up in his sedan outside of a REMAX real estate office and barges inside.

A tall, peerless woman, looks like she's straight out of *Desire Magazine,* and wearing a nametag which reads ROCHELLE HUNTER, answers the buzzer. Banks saunters into her office. She's Real Estate person of the week adept, although unraveled by Rude Buay's presence,

"I'm Rochelle Hunter. Who do I have the pleasure of finding their dream home today?"

Rochelle states, while directing Rude Buay to a seat.

"I'm Randy Bascombe."

"What brings you to *REMAX*, Mr. Bascombe?"

She asks,

Rude Buay responds,

"I'm very intrigued by your properties. I am looking for something very modish."

Rochelle responds,

"What's your interest? Mr. Bascombe, and what can we help you to move into within the next ninety days?"

Rude Buay is captivated by her beauty. Even so, he tries to conceal that desire.

Rude Buay replies,

"I'm looking for something Colonial with much privacy maybe. I'd like to be able to entertain my friends, well, ... *there*."

Rochelle replies,

"We're out of those colonials but there's a nice Victorian on the market right now. It's an entertainer's dream and privately tucked away in one of the most chic locations in Dade County. This impressive 3 acre new estate will have you staying for a long time. Private and gated entrance, sprawling lawn areas for volley ball, basketball, an adjacent tennis court, organic gardens, artist retreat and detached guest house. Mr. Bascombe, the ground floor plan offers 5 bedroom suites, great natural light, his study, her study as well as a craft room. A professional theater, billiards room, an extensive wine cellar, full size gym, and much more. Fit for a King!"

Rude Buay removes the Polaroid from his jacket, walks over to her desk, sits on its edge and lays them out in front Rochelle. She browses through.

Rude Buay says,

"I'd like one just like that or similar."

Rochelle reflects on that particular sale, as she scans through the database.

Rochelle states,

"Six months ago. Three million dollars! That's a rare one."

Rude Buay asks,

"Who's the proud owner?"

Rochelle responds,

"That's strictly confidential Mr. Bascombe."

"Really?"

Rude Buay inquires.

Rochelle informs,

"We are not under obligation to give out confidential information to potential buyers."

Rude Buay remarks,

"Could you have the owners give me a tour, just in case they ever decide to sell?"

Rochelle replies,

"Not on this one! We could have one like that built for you. It will take years..."

Rude Buay insists, still sitting on the edge of her desk.
Have you ever been...?
Rochelle questions,
"Why did you ask?"
Rude Buay pulls out his gun, pointing it towards her head.
She's trembling.
Rude Buay continues,
"I need a name and the address."
Rochelle retrieves the data from her rolodex.
Alberto Gomez. 712 Palm Grove.
Bang! Bang! Bang!
Bullet shells scatter throughout the office.
Several rounds of bullets through the glass window strike Rochelle.
Meanwhile Rude Buay ducks for cover. Lying on the ground he gets a few rounds off at the perpetrator. The villain Frankie is unhurt, as nothing connects owing to his agility.
Frankie speeds away from the scene inside the black limousine, his gun occupying the front passenger seat.
Rude Buay gets up, dusts himself off, darts outside boards his sedan, and follows aggressively in the pursuit of *One Arm Frankie*.
The fast driving *One Arm Frankie* eludes Rude Buay as his limo disappears in the distance.

Agent Rude Buay radios DEA Headquarters for backup while he continues in his pursuit of the culprit, Frankie O'Neal.

9

On top of a hill Rude Buays' vision is suckered into the much sought after Colonial Manor. Its grandeur is a majestic sight to behold. He is poised for this dream come true and the grand tour. Except that now it's *officially* DEA business. Finally, the most desired house is now less than a half mile away. His adrenaline rush is at an all-time high.

Rude Buay reaches inside his breast pocket and retrieves the blood stained Polaroid. He very quickly discerns that it's a perfect match. He radios DEA Headquarters for backup.

Miles Tate responds.

"I am coming up the hill. After you left I went to work and found the info on the house you were looking for. It is owned by Alberto Gomez. It is one of a kind. Very rare..."

"Enough! Tate. Just meet me there ASAP."

Says Rude Buay,

Tate speeds up. His sedan swerves as it careens through the narrow uphill streets. The Manor is now in sight. Tate, realizing that it's his first day on the job he *Man* up for the task ahead.

MOMENTS LATER, RUDE BUAY steps out of his car. Tate pulls up behind him and does likewise.

Rude Buay is confronted with multiple gate entries to inside the Manor. He presses the buzzer outside the huge Iron Gate to the manor while Tate covers.

There's no response.

So he tries again, unfortunately to no avail. Rude Buay relocates. He detects a switch box behind the Iron Gate.

He squeezes his hand through between the gate and the wall and PRIES open the box. The device: harnessed with not only multiple colored wires but an excess of black, blue and red wires.

Rude Buay is puzzled by the sophisticated wiring of the switch box. However, being occupied with bridging the buzzer with his device takes precedence.

While Tate focuses on keeping any possible retaliation at bay. Immediately, two Guards march out from the house toward the gate trigger happy.

Tate is alerted and ready. While they train their weapons, Tate counterattacks.

Tate CAPS both of them before they could accomplish their objective. With the two guards dead Rude Buay gives more of his attention to bridging the connection to the intercom. Yet, he remains unaccomplished.

The Black Limo PULLS up from the opposite direction, with full beamed illuminated headlights. Out of the limo RUSHES, Johnny *Too Bad*, and his partner Frankie O'Neal.

They immediately discharge multiple rounds at Tate and Rude Buay.

The agents retaliate trying to MATCH Frankie's onslaught and Johnny's fire power.

A smaller adjacent gate opens as if by its own accord.

Johnny and Frankie swiftly make their way through that gate while dodging the bullets from the agents' onslaught, as if they were the size of an NBA basketball. The gate closes abruptly behind them.

Rude Buay, peripherally notices the infrared on the surveillance camera up ahead. He aims, and SHOOTS at the camera, dismantling it. With the camera now out of commission. Johnny and Frankie's shooting intensifies as they REFUSE to let up.

Tate in the meantime, hides and shoots from behind the left wall pillar which supports the huge Iron Gate. Rude Buay does the SAME from behind the right pillar.

Rude Buay, in an effort to limit the Drug Lord's possible getaway tactics, SHOOTS up the black limo, deflating all four of its tires with his rounds of fire.

Tate single-handedly manages to keep Johnny and Frankie at bay, during a fierce, fiery, DEBRIS FLYING exchange caused by a sequence of RAINING bullets. Bullets, sailing through and over the iron gates from all the parties involved. Yet nothing connects.

Suddenly Frankie realizes that his gun's out of bullets.

Rude Buay clues in and aims for Frankie's head.

Frankie turns to flee.

Rude Buay SHOOTS.

Frankie somersaults. The bullet ricochets and catches Frankie in the left leg.

Frankie falls to the ground and gets back up limping and tossing rocks at the agents.

Johnny hurriedly reaches under his coat and with his right hand BRINGS out a semi-automatic. Now two gun - equipped, he does a 360 degree turn while he UNLOADS on Tate and Rude Buay.

The gun in Johnny's left hand goes CLICK, CLICK. He THROWS it to the ground and BRINGS out another with his left hand from under the left side of his coat as he continues to shoot with the one in his right hand.

During the swift exchange of this gun fire interim, Tate DARTS through flying bullets. He SPRINTS towards the limo and opens the rear door. Johnny sees the move made by Tate but he concentrates on TAKING OUT Rude Buay who is still attacking with a vengeance.

The wall pillar begins to sag as the Iron Gate moves a few inches horizontally, leaving a wider gap.

Rude Buay senses the pending collapse of the Iron Gate but RELOADS and continues shooting at Frankie and Johnny.

The Limo is penetrated with multiple bullet holes. Tate searches inside and discovers a collection of Uzis, grenades and other weaponry, in addition to several milk cans. Tate exchanges his semi-automatic for two Uzis and EXITS like *Rambo* in full force.

Tate DISCHARGES from both Uzis. Still he's no match for Johnny's experience and firing power, although unscathed by Johnny's onslaught.

Johnny yells out,

"Catch me if you can, Rude Buay!"

Rude Buay emerges from behind the twisted pillar and gets a glimpse at Frankie's and Johnny *Too Bad's* backside. He aims for Johnny *Too Bad*. However, they immediately disappear inside the interior of the Manor. The two agents with enough room barely

SQUEEZE their way through the partially opened gate. They enter the grounds very cautiously in pursuit.

The agents enter the gigantic living room by way of the front door. The ceiling's almost twelve feet high. A gigantic fire place with ash residue greets them. The Living room's decorated with oriental rugs and other elegant furniture. A large glass screen door leads to the pool area. There seems to be no current activity on the part of the dwellers, except for the incongruent display of blood stains.

Moving through each room in "take-down" style, looking for a trace of consistency, they wind up in the dining room. Next door is a bath room.

They search inside the bath room, no one's there. The table inside the dining room catches their attention. So they revert back to it.

Entering the dining room, they careen by the huge dining table, with twelve disheveled arranged chairs, and a bar secluded in the far corner. On the table: two huge partially fresh mounds of cocaine with two straws and two razor blades reside, refilled cigarettes, a pile of laced cigarette extracts, a crack pipe, syringes, and several Polaroid shots with groups of Asian kids.

Next to those pictures are opened milk cans. The agents complete their sweep of the house room by room but they still come up empty handed as the dwellers have left the premises without any obvious exit trail. The agents, puzzled by their exit strategy, rummage through the Manor second time around collecting evidence and hoping for a blunder on the part of the Drug Lords, so they could *roast* them.

IN THE MEANTIME Alberto, Shelly and Johnny *Too Bad* vacate the premises using a trap door leading to the underground beneath the building's foundation.

The trio boards a black limo. Frankie is in the driver's seat. A trail of blood leads to the driver's door. Frankie who had stopped the bleeding at the house is unaware that he is bleeding again as blood continues to trickle down his trousers' leg.

The limo departs and arrives at a small dock. There, a 75 foot submarine surfaces and docks. Alberto, Shelly and Johnny *Too Bad* exit the limo and board the ship. Meanwhile, Frankie oversees as the Sailor unloads several kilos along with laden milk cans onto the waiting limo. Frankie O'Neal gets back inside the limousine. Limo drives off. The Sailor re-boards. Moments later, the submarine submerges and departs.

Frankie in pain drives to Milky Way. He gets out of the limo. He unlocks the back door to the building and unloads the milk cans into the warehouse. Blood droplets still accompany his every move. He is hurt but skillfully masks the pain. He gets back inside the limo and retrieves a milk can off the front seat. He opens it, takes out the *Ziploc* bag of cocaine from underneath the powdered milk. Now powdered milk is all over the front seat. In a sense of urgency he opens the bag of coke, creates a few lines on the dashboard and snorts them up as if to ease the pain. In added desperation he places some on the wound and whimpers as the substance unites with his flesh. Anyway, he feels like there has been some relief to his pain. Even so, he is high, in a daze and now unable to drive. So he parks the car curbside.

10

Back up DEA agents arrive swarming the exterior of the Manor. They yellow tape the premises. Sensing no need to stay, they depart. Meanwhile, deep in the interior of the Manor Rude Buay hears a sound coming from the pool area. So he conducts another sweep of the premises with Tate covering him. Exiting through the rear door towards the pool they encounter a caged PARROT, too quiet for its own good.

Rude Buay entertaining the bird asks,

"You want a banana?"
The articulate Parrot yells,
"Thieves! Thieves! Thieves!"
Rude Buay convincingly,
"No we're not."
The Parrot not believing a word he says argues,
"Liars! Liars! Liars!"
Rude Buay questions,
"Undercover?"
The Parrot argues,
"Same thing! What's with the gun? Who'd you shoot,
Osahma? Bang, Bang, Bang, Bang!"
Rude Buay probes,
"Self-defense, that's all. Where's Alberto, Johnny and
the rest of the gang. Where did they go?
TATE is enjoying the exchange.
The Parrot responds,
"That's confidential!"
Rude Buay urges,
"Come on stud, I'll give you a peanut."
Parrot does a dance.
After the imaginary curtain, the parrot unveils,
"Sailing. Sail away."
Rude Buay feeds it another peanut and asks,
"How they do that?"
Rude Buay inquires.
Parrot responds,
"Trap door opens up! Ship sails!"

Rude Buay removes the cage and its occupant. Suddenly, the alarm for the building goes off. The sound of siren fills the air. Even so, Tate leads the way holding on to the bag of confiscated evidence. Rude Buay exits the house with the caged bird.

The Miami Police arrive in response to the alarm. Police cruisers swarm the grounds. Tate flashes his DEA badge.

"Miles Tate. DEA business."

Rude Buay in confrontation,

"Where the hell you were when we needed you?"

One of the Officers responds,

"Better late than never."

Rude Buay and Tate jump into their respective vehicles. Rude Buay, carries the caged bird. The vocal Miami Police Officer eyeing the caged parrot warns.

Officer continues,

"That's stolen property agent Rude Buay."

Rude Buay argues,

"He's a witness."

Parrot addresses,

"Where's the subpoena? I no see nada nor hear nada.

The vocal Miami police officer, somewhat amused, reaches for the bird. Could the parrot have been the witness to a getaway, knows the escape route in the house or just possess a vivid imagination? These thoughts lingered in Rude Buay's mind.

Anyway, he reluctantly hands over the bird to the Miami Police Officer.

Rude Buay feeling a hunch says,

"You can hold onto the bird but cover the exterior; or your A… is mine."

The Officer doesn't seem to get it.

Rude Buay continues,

"I have some unfinished business to complete on the inside. We will call you if I need you."

Rude Buay returns to the interior of the house with Miles Tate following in tow.

Inside the Manor Rude Buay eyes every square foot of the floor looking for anything that resembles a crack in the rug and carpet. From room to room he surveys. Inside the master bathroom which they previously visited, they come up upon a rectangular crease in the rug. The rectangular outline in the carpet indicates that a door, the size of a trap door is concealed in it. The agents tug on the carpet. A door opens up in the floor of the bathroom floor. Engaging the descending steps, with their guns cocked the two agents wind up inside the partially lit tunnel.

Descending inside the tunnel agent Rude Buay and Miles Tate discover several luxurious, expensive automobiles. In an investigative pursuit they notice cars are parked on one end. The other end leads through a thoroughfare with a fork. The two agents walk the full length of the small tunnel which opens into a small dock.

11

Rude Buay notices the fresh tire marks left in the mud next to the dock. Additionally, blood stains create a trail at the scene. Rude Buay "rolls up his sleeves" and calculates the measurement of the vehicles chassis based on the impressions of the tire marks most dominant and resident in the mud. Based on his calculations he estimates that this vehicle had to be at least 120 inches or more in length.

Staring across at the blue watered horizon, he adds yet another piece to the getaway puzzle.

"So this is where they made their escape."

Rude Buay declares,
Miles Tate responds,
 "Sure looks like it!"
Rude Buay nods yes.
Miles Tate inquires,
"So what's next?"
Rude Buay, thinks long and hard as if he is not quite up to it. Then looking at Tate with direct eye contact he responds,
"The Caribbean! If it's going to be up to me."
Miles Tate responds,
"Lies, corruption, deceit and sabotage. Some trip huh?"
Rude Buay looking across the horizon responds,
"You've got to be in it to win it. Before the Caribbean though, I need to pick up some milk."
Miles Tate questions,
"Really? Milk?"
Rude Buay answers,
"Yep! Milk!"

IN SEPARATE DEA CARS the agents drive through Miami, passing several supermarkets.
Tate doesn't get Rude Buay's epiphany so he radios Rude Buay.
"You forgot to get the milk?"
Tate asks,

"No I didn't. Just stay on my tail and don't shoot unless I say so."

Rude Buay advises,

Moments later the duo pulls up at Milky Way.

The Black limousine driven by Frankie pulls away from the curb. Rude Buay recognizes Frankie and vice versa. Rude Buay is in pursuit followed by Tate.

The race proceeds through the streets of Miami.

Frankie tries to make a getaway before the entrance to Interstate 95 Freeway. Rude Bauy is tailing him closely so he changes his mind and opts for the highway's ramp. The two agents pursue resolutely.

Rude Buay radios Tate.

"Get ready, I rather have him alive than dead."

Tate questions,

"What's his value?"

Rude Buay informs his rookie,

"He didn't lose that one arm for nothing. I am sure."

Rude Buay tunes to his favorite reggae station. The DJ is playing his favorite. The vibe soothes.

Rude Buay instructs Tate via other radio,

"Call Headquarters and request a search and seizure at the Milky Way Warehouse, will you?"

The Limousine merges with traffic as it enters the HOV lane. The two agents' vehicles follow suit.

They are now keeping pace with the limo. That dancehall music is still playing as if it's an extended version. Frankie, sensing being tailgated, exits the

HOV lane illegally and merges all the way to the right, thus causing a multi vehicle collision while making his getaway. Rude Buay skillfully avoids the mayhem, while Tate is boxed in because of the related accident.

Rude Buay continues in pursuit of Frankie. The chase escalates through city streets, where the maneuvering of this 120 inch stretch limo is now problematic at such a high speed, thereby posing a problem for other motorists as well.

On-lookers see a fatality brewing as pedestrians and motorist use their cell phones to video tape the happenings. Catching Frankie alive would appease Rude Buay but in his mind, not at the expense of the lives of other motorists.

Suddenly, bullets from the limousine begin to rain in the direction of Rude Buay's sedan. Rude Buay aims for the right rear tire and connects.

The limo swerving from side to side, careens, slams into a retaining wall, lands on its roof and bursts into flames.

Rude Buay gets out of his vehicle in an attempt to observe the demolition. Meanwhile, Tate pulls up, gets out of his sedan, and stares at the flames and then back at Rude Buay.

Tate asks,

"I thought we wanted him alive."

Rude Buay replies,

"In life you go after what you want, but there is nothing wrong about accepting what you get. The thrill lies in the effort."

Tate looks at Rude Buay while assimilating that thought. He begins buying in to Rude Buay's positive mental attitude.

Rude Buay asks,

"Are you still up for the Caribbean?"

Tate smiles and responds,

"I wouldn't renege on the Caribbean for anything in the world."

They board their vehicles and depart back to DEA headquarters. Agent Tate is excited and enthused about going to the Caribbean.

12

R ude Buay is in his office typing an email. He later submits it addressed to Michael Ortiz. Walking out of the parking garage, Ortiz retrieves the email via his cell phone. He senses the importance, knowledgeable of the fact that it's not really Rude Buay's style to send him an Email.

Ortiz mulls over the contents as he knocks on Rude Buay's office door. Rude Buay answers the door. Ortiz barges in, and looks squarely at Rude Buay in the face.

Immediately, two junior agents enter through the still open office door. Both agents are laden with part of the seizure recovered from their Milky Way drug bust.

One of the agent's remarks, while focusing one of the milk containers:

"That place has recently turned into a narcotics depot. I don't think any place in Asia, Colombia, Canada, Mexico or even the Caribbean has been this busy lately when it comes to narcotics trafficking. We just lost agent Jones, he was a good man. It is going to be necessary to put Milky Way under surveillance 24/7."

Ortiz responds paying attention to the email and then to Rude Buay.

"Rude Buay, you've been there before. The U.S. did them a huge favor by extraditing Johnny *Too Bad* from Jamaica. That should have helped. It's about time the locals fight their own narcotics war."

Rude Buay responds,

"So said your predecessor the deceitful agent Jose Mendez. This is our war. If we lose this one, we could be in for one of the most tragic recalls this world has ever encountered – Milk.

The prison authorities did the locals a huge disfavor by setting Johnny free.

With a menace of that caliber on the loose, who knows what will happen next? Who knows what his next target will be?

Our freedom gets eroded every day. Mainly, because we fail to be all we can be.

To know something is wrong and not do anything about it is worse than not knowing that thing is wrong."

Agent Rude Buay looks over at the junior agents and continues.

"Let me set the record straight. If you feel so sentimental about Milky Way, maybe you should step out of your comfort zones: by honing your skills so you could protect your love interest."

They both make their exit feeling agitated regarding Rude Buays' sentimentalism statement.

Ortiz saving face,

"Rude Buay, give me until tomorrow to come to a decision. You understand that we are short staffed. Who knows when agent Heidi Hudson will be well enough to return to active duty?"

Rude Buay reminds,

"Boss, the clock has been ticking since that submarine sailed from the Miami dock.

Let me remind you: The most notorious Drug Lord since Alberto Gomez is on the loose.

Not only that, he has also linked up with Alberto and his name is Johnny *Too Bad*.

Who knows what the two politicians could be concocting?

I will be packed and ready to go in the morning.

This is my country and they are my people.
If not Me?
Who?"
If not Now?
When?"

13

It's late evening in Shanghai, China. *Femme Fatales* Denise Gomez, Shelly Hall and Amanda Kinsley show up outside the Shanghai Karate School. The women are all dressed in karate gear, accessorized by luggage including duffle bags. They survey and wait. Suddenly, David Lee gets off the elevator. The women are alerted as he turns the corner inside the lobby.

They unzip the duffel bags and remove their semi-automatic weapons. The dark alley behind them adds to the grittiness and the pre-nightfall.

David steps onto the sidewalk and is confronted with three women and three weapons pointing directly at him as they sucker him inside a portion of the dark alley.

In high flying Kung Fu style David single-handedly disarms all three women leaving them defenseless. Even so, they remain verbally confrontational.

"This is not right, David...!"

Denise yells,

"Don't blame me, blame Sal. He cuts and package..."

David responds.

"What does Sal have to do with this? This is a tough economy. Recession is eating away at our profit margin. Thankfully we've got milk, that's our only conduit. Your packaging is horrendous that's why we...."

Denise explains.

"Do you know what could happen if milk gets recalled?"

Shelly interjects.

"Kids will starve."

David Lee replies.

"So would we!"

Denise responds.

"How many containers were in your last shipment?"

Denise asks.

"One thousand cans..."

David responds,

"One Thousand Cans?"

Denise, Shelly and Amanda questioningly interrupt.

"That's what I said. One Thousand one-eight Kilos,"

David restates.

"We are going to have to use a different vendor for our containers, bags and cans. That's not our style. It is all about quality. That is our entire existence."

David continues.

"Too late. Too ... LATE! No wonder you flunked out of high school, you bozo. What else have you fell short on? Those *Ziploc* bags are defective."

States Shelly Hall,

Denise reminds David.

"My husband pays you well. Not for a botch job."

"This is my living. Yes I flunked High School. If there is no me you don't eat. Plus wear that expensive jewelry."

Shelly attempts to retrieve her gun from the ground. David senses her move.

David remarks,

"You touch that gun and I will break your jawbone."

Denise looks across at Amanda. The Boss Woman Amanda clues in. Amanda shows David the snake.

He responds with the crane.

They go at it hand to hand combat, Kung Fu style, with Amanda gaining the upper hand. When it was all over, David lies on the sidewalk not only exhausted, but badly hurt, "licking his wounds and totally embarrassed."

His lady, CHU LING, an Asian model in her late 20s, pulls up in her fully loaded BMW. She steps out, glides across and onto the sidewalk peering inside the dark alley.

As a result of the humiliation and the pain endured by her man, the take-out order of Chinese food Chu's carrying, falls out of her hands and onto the paved sidewalk in decorativeness.

Denise, ignoring Chu's presence, responds sarcastically as the three of them leave the scene,

"Take that! Get your act together or next time or you will experience a threesome."

14

The following morning, Michael Ortiz walks inside Rude Buay's office and notices he's all packed with Tate's luggage aligned next to his. Tate walks in and in acknowledgement of his superiors, he smiles accompanied by a slight nod of the head.

Ortiz addresses:

"Your return to Miami is very much anticipated gentlemen. Who knows where the next tunnel will be constructed. Our city needs you now more than ever."

Rude Buay and Ortiz shake hands. Rude Buay and agent Tate leaves in a sedan. Tate takes the wheel.

On the drive to the airport, Rude Buay catches up on making some phone calls.

He dials.

Inside the gadget filled living room WALTER BANKS, an African American man with salt and pepper hair and in his fifties is on the phone. On the other cell phone, in Bogota, Colombia, is a barefooted CHELO, in his mid-30s and of Colombian decent. Chelo secures a newly constructed ladder to a tree overlooking the village, and mainly its long stretch of dusty unpaved roadway.

"What is next for him and Johnny, nobody knows. I am sure if matters get worse Rude Buay will respond."

Walter Banks states,

"Did he ever pay you from that last…?"

Chelo asks,

Banks interrupts,

"Hold on Chelo, talk about the devil and here he is. I have to grab this call. Let's talk later."

Banks aborts that call with Chelo and facilitates Rude Buays'.

"Man after my own heart, Mr. Rude Buay! Chelo and I were just talking about you. When are you going to pay the homeland a visit? So we could enjoy some roast breadfruit, with *Ting*, ackee, and salt-fish."

"Don't tempt me with that finger licking food, Banks. You know how this black man loves to feed his stomach. As a matter of fact I will be there on the first flight in from Miami in the morning. Why don't you, Mildred and the Commissioner meet my partner Tate and me for a mid-day debriefing at the hole in the wall?"

"I don't foresee a problem with Mildred attending; you know how that woman feels about you. On the other hand, the General Election talks are heating up, not sure about the Commissioner, but one never knows if he will be able to meet with you on such a short notice."

The sedan pulls up at the airport parking lot. Rude Buay is still on the phone.

"Banks, 9:00 a.m., see you then."

Banks calls MILDRED SIMMS a Caribbean beauty in her late twenties. Mildred is filing her nails at the office. She is a drop dead gorgeous, sophisticated African American beauty, every man's heart desire. She picks up on the second ring.

"Mr. Banks ah whey yo ah deal with?"

She answers in deep *patois*.

Banks somewhat taken aback as he had never heard Mildred drop some *patois* before.

"Rude Buay will be in tomorrow. He wants to meet at noon at the hole in the wall. Are you available…?"

"Is that doctor going to be there?"

Inquires Mildred,

"It's a dpiuiuyt ebrief…"

Banks responds.

"Okay, will you come get me?"

Mildred suggests.

"Will do!"

Says Banks.

RICHARD BAPTISTE, the commissioner is sitting across from the Governor General Bradford Wiley. The two men are casting light on the Beverly Hastings situation. Wiley suggests that Beverly be reunited with her four kids. Based on the fact that she was unaware the milk was contaminated with cocaine.

On the other hand, Baptiste feels that the situation should not be rushed. Additionally, he argues that Beverly should be retested for any possibility she was under the influence at the time of Leticia's death or has recently been a narcotics user.

Baptiste's office phone rings. He gets it.

"Mr. Commissioner, its Walter Banks!"

Baptiste accommodates.

"I know you are a busy man. Mr. Rude Buay will be coming in tomorrow. He will be arriving at 9:00 a.m. Rude Buay would like to meet at noon, to catch up on old times, and the current crisis, if you are available."

"Oh Really? You mean that he did this on his own accord. What a changed man! Tell him I will oblige. By the way do you know if that scorpion he had on his head is a temporary fixture or a permanent one?"

Baptiste inquires,

"You may want to ask him about that yourself. I am sure he will fill you in. See you at the hole in the wall, Commissioner."

Banks replies.

The Commissioner returns to his discussion with the Governor General.

While Walter Banks aborts the call and continues to enjoy the sunset view of the harbor.

15

The shadows lengthen as the sun sinks beyond the horizon in Montego Bay, Jamaica. Late workers enjoy the light flow of traffic as they leave their jobs for their respective domiciles. A few vagrants hang out at the corner streets. Some are getting high while others are just chilling listening to music via earphones on their iphones. A cargo van displaying U.S Diplomat licenses tags pulls up and parks on the outside next to the Ministry of Tourism building. Inside under the wheel is Shelly Hall,

Denise is upfront on the passenger seat, while Amanda is in the rear seat with her gun in hand.

A security guard notices the vehicle but fails to investigate; taking those diplomat plates for granted. In his mind it could be nothing more than a UN diplomat, conducting official business. Workers continue to file out of the Ministerial compound, some pedestrians and motorists, carpoolers as well.

Mildred Simms steps out of the building and travels towards her car. That stud of a security guard steps out of the booth and walks over to her. He sneakily indulges in walking her to her car. She gets inside. He closes the door behind her. The car takes off.

Mildred drives out of the parking lot. Suddenly, her car is sandwiched by three other cars one in-front and two behind.

The diplomat wearing tag van is now several cars behind Mildred's car and tailing it.

Approaching a small street, Shelly Hall notices the right indicator light blinking on Mildred's car up above. Mildred pulls up next to a hair salon. She parks the car, gets out of her car. She is heading towards the salon.

The van speeds up and stops parallel to Mildred's car. Mildred is sandwiched. Denise and Amanda jump out while Shelly completes the parking of the van.

Denise immediately stalls Mildred as she steps out. Amanda, with gun in one hand wraps a huge bath towel continuously around Mildred's head. Tying a knot where the fabric ends.

Mildred's scream is almost muffled under the towel.

They drag her to and inside of the van.

The van takes off as they finish binding her with ropes. They remove the towel and duct tapes over Mildred's mouth.

Simultaneously, Johnny is positioned in a cube truck a few hundred feet away from the Commissioners' home in MO Bay. Johnny *Too Bad* waits.

Secluded in a classy suburban neighborhood, not only very little evening traffic, but the chirping noise of crickets accompany Johnny's' linger.

The Commissioner's car pulls up. Richard Baptiste, always a sharp dresser. He is suited with a nice shirt and tie. He looks suave and debonair. No doubt happy to be home after a long day at the office. His car stops, waiting on a lounging cat to clear its leisurely stroll across the street. Baptiste prepares to pull into the driveway.

Johnny takes off in the cube truck and intentionally rear ends the Commissioner's car.

The Commissioner gets out peeved, as he evaluates the damage done to this car.

Johnny steps out as if to console the Commissioner and possibly exchange some vehicular documental information. Instead Johnny displays his gun. He puts Commissioner Baptiste under a choke hold, sticks a rag deep in his mouth, escorts him to the rear of the truck, opens it, and shoves him inside. Johnny duct-tapes the Commissioner's mouth, closes the door, returns to the driver's seat and takes off.

Now underway, Johnny radios Alberto.

"Mission accomplished, Boss!"

Albert responds,

"Let's meet up in Port Antonio close to the MPs blockade. Stay put once you get there. I will drive to meet you."

Johnny responds in *patois*,

"Scene, Rasta! I love those Ministers of Parliament to … *rarted*."

16

Outside Walter Banks' Port Antonio home a taxi pulls up and waits. Under the wheel sits Drug Czar and leader of the Dragon Drug Cartel, Alberto Gomez. Meanwhile, inside Walter Banks' house, the house phone rings. Banks answers it on the second ring.

On the other end is Chelo his Colombian understudy. He's sitting on his living room floor in Bogota, Colombia toying with his espionage gadgets. He picks up a video signal from Walter Banks neighborhood in Jamaica.

"Banks there's a taxi waiting on your block. Did you call a blue taxi cab? Are you going someplace? Did Rude Buay show up earlier than planned?"

Chelo is now affixed to the TV monitor, and images of the blue cab. He zooms in for more clarity.

Finally the monitor goes blank.

Chelo fiddles with a few gadget antennas while he's still talking on the phone.

"I saw that taxi outside your home. The driver just sat there waiting. Your house lights were on. So I figured you were at home. Now I lost that … signal. I don't see it anymore. Let me try fixing the signal router. I will call you back."

Banks' phone rings again.

It's Chelo,

"Sorry Banks no more picture. I lost it. I saw it a few minutes ago. Conyo! The blue taxi cab was there. I did not get the driver's profile though. He looked … It happened so fast."

"Is he black? What does he look like?"

Banks inquires as he grabs his gun.

"Not sure. I didn't get a close up of the driver. The image was just a flicker"

Chelo responds.

"Darn, if Rude Buay changed his itinerary, why didn't he inform me? He knows where I stand with surprises. I hate them. He better not … pulling one on me. I'll blow his brains out."

Banks states as he ensure that his gun is fully loaded.

"If he did, that's a big NO. Even if he offers you a bonus, you just never know with those Americans."

"Got picture! Got Picture!"

Yells Chelo.

Continuing,

"It looks like the Don. Don Alberto it is. He just stepped out of the taxi."

Banks finally gets picture. It reveals Alberto coming toward the house, and carrying a sack large enough to house an UZI.

FLASHBACK:

Rude Buay calls a taxi and leaves. Later, Banks is sitting at the table at home having coffee while he reviews blueprint. Suddenly, a bullet coming through his glass window pane strikes him. He blacks out.

BACK TO PRESENT:

Seeing this, Banks, knowing that an UZI will outmatch his arsenal of weaponry, he turns off the light and exits through the back door, carrying his cell phone and semi-automatic gun in hand.

Alberto shows up outside the house. He removes the UZI from the sack, attached with a silencer. He knocks on the front door. There's no answer. He blows out he lock and enters the house. He switches the light on and rummages from room to room. There is no Walter Banks.

Noticing Banks espionage gadgets, he kicks most of them over in addition to unplugging the multiple TV monitors.

Meanwhile, Banks dials 911 for emergency backup before returning to the house, just in case he confronted Alberto. The Don Alberto sees Banks' shadow entering the yard. He unloads several rounds on the Jamaican agent. Nothing connects. Banks fires back also missing the agile Alberto. The neighbors are alerted by the sound of firearms. Suddenly, the once quiet neighborhood except for the sound of ships is awakened to the sound of gun shots like popping corn.

Alberto gets inside the taxi and drives away before the community could converge on him.

Moments later, late arriving Jamaican police flood the area in squad cars. They are too late. Alberto has already fled the area.

Chelo, losing signal once again in that satellite unfriendly community of Port Antonio is unable to capture Alberto's getaway.

Alberto Gomez later abandons the car in a ravine and joins forces with his partner in crime, Johnny *Too Bad*. Together they drive away with the Commissioner, taking him hostage.

17

The shaken up Walter Banks, nevertheless shows up solo and on time to meet with Rude Buay and Rude Buay's partner Miles Tate. Rude Buay greets Banks and then introduces him to agent Miles Tate.

"Glad to know you've escaped."

Says Rude Buay.

"Thanks to Chelo, and his high tech gadgets. His work will no doubt be in the Smithsonian Institute someday."

Banks replies,

"The Dragon Drug Cartel's MO indicates that they were planning a clean sweep operation. By kidnapping Mildred, the Commissioner and then you, they would not have only left us ill-equipped to compete effectively - totally short staffed to combat their onslaughts."

A waitress seats the three men at a table.

Rude Buay asks,

"Which of the locals do you confide in, and can be made ready soon?"

"Not sure about that. Most are still upset how America handled the extradition of Johnny *Too Bad*.

States Walter Banks,

"Ah, they should let sleeping dogs lie. The man is a menace, always has been."

Interjects agent Tate,

"Banks we will find the kidnappers along with the members of your team. 'We may lose some battles but rest assured we will win this war.'

Rude Buay cleverly responds.

The waitress serves up some roast breadfruit *ting* and salt fish with ackee. Tate looks as if he is not sure about the food.

Rude Buay in confidence,

"Eat up man it's all good. *Ital* food! Don't bite your fingers when you are finished."

Tate obliges and is relishing the savory dish.

Banks interjects,

"Maybe the doctor will, seeing she knows so much about our last mission."
Rude Buay responds,
"I am afraid it's not her thing. They said if little Leticia was able to get to the hospital on time her life might have been spared."
"The doctor is that good huh?"
Tate responds.
"Yes Tamara is great at what she does."
Claims Rude Buay,
"Do we get to...?"
Tate interjects as he is interrupted by Banks.
"Yes, there is a great spot we can go after sunset."
"I haven't had a chance to talk with DEA headquarters about these kidnappings along with other new developments. By sunset the kidnappers could be asking for ransoms,"
States agent Rude Buay.
"You think?"
Tate replies,
"... and after sunset no partying?"
Says Banks.
Rude Buay responds,
'I'd like to ask for a rain-check on that one."
"You could invite TAMARA. Its Jamaica, got to mix business with a little bit of pleasure. You never know who is connected to..."
Rude Buay reflects.

"Agent Tate is too wet behind the ears to deflect."
Banks inserts,
"Plus he is missing his tattoo."
Tate looks across at both men in response,
"I must say that I have read the entire account. I love it!"
"Good! I don't want to have to take you fishing for Jacks."
"Is Jacks your favorite fish?"
Tate asks.
"Every snitch finds out the hard way."
Rude Buay states as he excuses himself from the table.
Tate follows Rude Buay.
While Banks stays behind.

18

At the Crows' Nest, an upscale restaurant nestled between the coconut trees and the beach in MO BAY. Rude Buay, Tate and Banks are at a table having a few drinks. There is one vacant chair across from Rude Buay. The soulful reggae artist performs a combination of dancehall favorites and ballads.

The three men are enjoying the ambience of the revelry.

TAMARA ROSS, the stunningly eye-catching, 26-year-old beauty walks in. She has never looked so hot publicly. Eyes in the semi-lit room are focused on her, multiple double takes, indicated by the turning of the necks from all genders. If a massage therapist was present, that individual was about to cash in big time with some deep tissue and double sessions.

Rude Buay acknowledges Tamara while admiring her sensuality.

Rude Buay gets up from his seat, pulls out her chair. She sits.

He slides that chair in a little closer to the table.

Tamara is flattered.

He pats her lightly on the shoulder area.

She smiles.

He responds in kind.

Rude Buay introduces her,

"Glad you could join us. This is my partner agent Miles Tate. Agent Tate, meet Dr. Tamara Ross."

Tate, drinking Guinness Stout, possibly for the first time could not contain himself. The bottled drink slips out of Tate's hand and spills in the direction of Walter Banks, some splattering on Banks' evening attire.

"Sorry, my gosh. I am so sorry."

Banks responds,

"Hey, calm down, you only had half of the bottle. What is the matter...?"

Rude Buay interjects,

"I don't think it's the drink. Maybe..."

The *Maître D.* darts in with a mop and wash rag. He begins cleaning up the spill.

The waiter aids him while he evacuates the guests to a table close to the stage.

The artist delivers another hot number. Tamara wishing Rude Buay will do this dance.

Even so, all eyes at the table are focused on Miles Tate.

Tamara, the lady she is, has been somewhat taken aback by Tates' naivety.

Banks looks at the ruin caused to his "Threads."

Rude Buay jesters,

"Tate is so on top of his game he memorized our last account verbatim in less than a day."

Banks stares at Tate in amazement.

Rude Buay continues,

"He said if he was going to be efficient he needed to prepare himself by learning from those who have gone through the minefield against the Dragon Drug Cartel. But he still has a lot to prove...'

Tamara interjects,

"Don't be so hard on him Rude Buay. Tate you are going to love it here in Jamaica. Watch out for those *Hotties!*"

Tate regains his presence of mind and addresses Dr. Ross,

"Thanks. So how does that voodoo works? Is the lighting of the candle and creating a periphery a part of the ritual? Or that is just something you do? "

Dr. Ross responds,

"It doesn't matter, light or no light a circle or a square, it's all in the belief mechanism. You can if you believe you can."

Tate focuses in on Rude Buay, who responds:

"Never practiced, don't care for its workings."

The artist takes a break and the DJ spins some vinyl.

Suddenly, a woman in her late 50s, wearing a head tie shows up at the table. She interrupts. In Rude Buay's mind sight he visualizes Maude Davis, his long gone godmother.

The woman hands Rude Buay a folded piece of paper, and departs. Rude Buay opens it. The others are ignorant in regard to what's contained therein.

It says:

"Your friends are in Tivoli Gardens, West Kingstown. Seek and you shall find. Knock and it shall be opened unto you. Ask and it shall be given onto you."

Immediately, Rude Buay's phone rings.

He answers.

It's his boss Michael Ortiz.

"Rude Buay, I have some great news, Heidi Hudson has been reactivated. She will resume active duty tomorrow, and team up with you and Tate in Jamaica. Now promise me one thing. All three of your asses will be coming back alive to Miami when this is all over."

Rude Buay responds,

"Great move! That second part I can't promise though. It has much to do with the playing of the hand versus the one that's been dealt."

All eyes at that table are fixed on agent Rude Buay. They all anticipate him breaking the news.

He does,

"Hudson will be joining us in the morning!"

"That is awesome!"

Says Tamara.

She continues,

"Now I don't have to spend my night at the shooting range."

Banks jokingly,

"I won't be surprised if you are strapped right now."

They all celebrate with cheers.

Moments later, they wrap the event.

Rude Buay takes Tamara up on a much celebrated night cap.

19

Outside the small airport hangar at Kingston Airport, agent HEIDI HUDSON, Caucasian, in her early thirties, wearing dark sunglasses and street clothes deplanes. Two full size minivans wait. Agent Rude Buay and Tate step out from the black minivan and Banks steps from the gray minivan. The three men greet agent Hudson. After which Rude Buay directs her to Walter Banks' vehicle. She gets inside.

The hatch of the aircraft opens up and with the aid of the pilot the three men load eclectic assortments

ammunition including UZIs and AK 45s into the rear
of both minivans.

The black and gray vehicles step into their low rider
modes and take off in "rhythm and soul through
Kingston."

Inside the gray minivan, Banks, under the wheel is
poised for battle. Hudson in the front passenger seat
though buckled in, she holds on for her dear life.

Banks reiterates,

"Welcome back agent Hudson."

Hudson replies,

"I love this place! I must say that things have changed
since our last visit. Do you think we are going to be
able to find Mildred and Baptiste with all the going
ons?"

"Where there is a will there is a way."

Banks continues,

"That's what agent Rude Buay believes."

Hudson responds,

"He is so resilient, charismatic and at times
untouchable. Rude Buay cares about his people so
much. It is contagious."

"We so appreciate him,"

Replies Banks.

Both vehicles are approaching West Kingston. Rude
Buay tunes the car radio to 100.9 FM Radio Jamaica.
The reggae music fades abruptly. The crisp articulate
announcer says: "We continue to follow information

regarding the death of the three year old Leticia Hastings who died of a cocaine overdose last week." Rude Buay presses the transmit button on the stereo, the gray minivan picks up the timely audio feed.

"News just in states: that over one million cartons of powdered milk are feared being recalled around the world, according to the FDA. This happened after a three year old girl lost her life as a result of being accidentally fed contaminated milk. It was alleged that a *Ziploc* bag containing almost one eight kilo of cocaine ruptured in a container of milk. Leticia was innocently fed the milk by her mother Beverly Hastings. Leticia died later as a result of that drug overdose.

In other related news, police commissioner and his one-time partner in crime Mildred Simms have still not been found after they were both kidnapped by alleged members of the Dragon Drug Cartel last week. Walter Banks a member of their team, it was reported survived kidnapped attempts by the cartel. Stay tuned for the weather forecast when we return."

With a mountainous backdrop the street sign reads: Approaching Tivoli Gardens.

Moments later, the two minivans roll into Tivoli Gardens. Gunmen on multiple rooftops are alerted. Even so, they are mesmerized by the hydraulic movements displayed by both vehicles. As a result, the vans proceed unscathed and with celebrated applause.

Rude Buay addresses his colleagues in the gray minivan via stereo.

"Our objective is to rescue the kidnapped. If blood is to be shed, let it be that of the kidnappers and not ours. We are a team. 'United we will stand. Divided we will certainly fall.' Our only burning desire is to win. Whatever it takes, remember, we all come out of this alive. Welcome to TG better known as Tivoli Gardens."

20

ack at the Commissioner's house, a Fed Ex package arrives. Christine Baptiste signs for it. The senders address seemed ineligible to her. Anyway, she opens it and discovers Richard's wallet. Inside the package she finds a note which reads: RB - RIP.

Christine rushes for her cell phone. She immediately calls Rude Buay, he answers the cellular phone call.

Rude Buay, this is Christine, Richards' wife. I know you are very busy but I was asked to update you in regard to the kidnapping of my husband Richard. A

package was just delivered to me by Fed Ex. In it were Richard's wallet and a note which reads: RB – RIP. Have you heard anything from the kidnappers? Did they mention anything about a ransom as yet?"
Rude Buay responds,
"We have not heard anything as of yet. As soon as or when we do, we will definitely inform you. Mrs. Baptiste, are those hidden cameras installed at your home working efficiently?"
In tears, Christine says,
"Yes! Thank you for making that possible."
The four agents continue on their quest through Tivoli Gardens.
Rude Buay asks agent Tate,
"What would you say are the three things that make you tick as a DEA?"
Miles Tate responds,
"Search, Seizure and Arrest, I'm still waiting for the latter … "
Many teens line the streets, buyers and sellers alike.
Rude Buay pulls up to the curb.
Banks follow suits and corners the sellers.
Hudson jumps out to assist.
Rude Buay chases after the Buyers.
Tate catches up and grabs one of the teens and confiscates several marijuana *spliffs*.
Rude Buay senses the potential buried inside the more than a dozen teens.

He addresses them,

"My name is agent Rude Buay and these are my colleagues. Don't ever let us see you all out here again."

The youths are released by the agents, and immediately vacate the area.

The agents return to their car. Tate is mesmerized by the giant size of these confiscated rolled in newspaper marijuana joints. He is tempted. Rude Buay looks across at him.

Rude Buay cautions:

"Not on my watch."

Tate changes that mindset.

Banks keeps up with Rude Buay. Agents Tate and Hudson get an eyeful of the weaponry displayed by some guards standing outside a wooded house. Rude Buay pulls up and stops in-front of the battalion. Tate is terrified.

"Are you okay?"

Asks the veteran agent - Rude Buay.

Without waiting for an answer Rude Buay says,

"Follow me,"

Banks and Hudson wait inside their greatly admired minivan.

Rude Buay asks the armed guards:

"Where is Levy? Need to see him."

One of the guards responds,

"Nobody sees Levy."

Rude Buay flashes his badge, pushes the guard out of the way, and barges in followed by Tate.

LEVY, is a bearded man in his 50s, wearing a knitted hat in the colors of the flag. His dreadlocks are rolled up underneath the black, yellow and green. There is a wide assortment of narcotics and money in the now entered living room of the house.

Levy greets.

"Hey Rude Buay, not because you are wearing a badge, it doesn't give you the right to barge in on I and I like that. *Chua*? Anyway, let's get down to business. What can I do for you, *mon*?

Rude Buay responds,

"I am looking for Mildred Simms and the Commissioner. I heard that Johnny has them."

"Who told you that?"

Asks Levy.

"Come on, you know that the commissioner helped in having him extradited to the U.S. If you were in his shoes: Who would be one of the first people to exercise vindictiveness upon? Plus his finger prints were found on the commissioner's vehicle after the kidnapping occurred."

"America has given Johnny a bad rap. We run things in Tivoli Gardens, and he might be referred to as Johnny *Too Bad* but he doesn't have your people. Plus you just touched my door with your bare hands on your way in. If I wanted to plant your finger prints at the scene of a crime, I can hire the experts to do so. Money is power and when you don't have any it not only stinks, it sours,"

Says Levy,

Rude Buay doesn't believe a word he says. Even so, he notices the AKA 45 sitting on Levy's table.

Meanwhile the guards on the outside of Levy's establishment focus on the waiting gray minivan with Banks and Hudson inside.

Rude Buay turns to leave.

Levy says,

"Happy Hunting!"

Rude Buay eyes Tate.

Tate draws and points his gun in Levy's face.

Levy asks,

"What is this Rude Buay, you didn't get what you wanted? You afraid of what the Jamaicans will do to you, so you are going to have the White Man shoot me."

Rude Buay responds,

"No I am not. I want answers."

Rude Buay grabs Levy in a choke hold. Drags him to the rest room and sticks his head deep down in the un-flushed toilet.

Rude Buay demands,

"Now are you going to tell me where my people are or do I have to make you drink first?"

Levy replies in hard core *patois*,

"That is I and I piss. No problem if *me* drink it. That would not resurrect your brother Clifford. Is harden him been harden!"

Rude Buay again demands'

"Give me a location. Do you want to live or you want to die?"

Rude Buay submerges Levy's head a second time into the toilet bowl, and then releases him.

Levy spits out a mouthful on Rude Buay.

Rude Buay punches him hard in the face. Levy rocks back. He launches a fist at Rude Buay. The agent ducks out of it and shoots Levy in the face.

Levy's *Posse* on the outside is alerted by the gun shot. In their mind they are thinking that Levy shot Rude Buay.

Rude Buay barges out with Tate behind him. The surprised guards try training their weapons on the agents. Banks and Hudson jump out of their vehicle in assistance to Rude Buay and Tate in the onslaught of the guards.

The death count at Levys' establishment equaled eleven, ten guards and Levy.

An old man, looking out his window from across the street, sees the body count. He yells from his window in some hard core *patois*,

"You looking fo Johnny? Him up at Chin Chins Bar and Grill, on Friday nights. Right up on Mannings Hill Road. *Me* hope you speak Chinese."

Rude Buay steps out, puts a Hundred dollar bill under a rock.

The old man clues in and hurries down to get it.

The four agents proceed to Chin Chins Bar and Grill.

21

The agents merge onto Kent Street and pull up next to Chin Chins. Rude Buay and Tate barge inside the bar and grill restaurant. Banks and Hudson wait outside in surveillance mode. It's dinner time inside Chin Chins. Some people are dining, some drinking, some just listening to music, others are shooting pool.

The agents survey, there is no glimpse of Johnny. Rude Buay walks up to the bar. The bartender, his name tag reads JIM, and is busy tending. So Rude Buay waits his turn.

"Hey Jim I am looking for Johnny, seen him lately?

"No *mon* sorry."

Bartender returns to his duty.

Tate yells at him,

"Seen or heard anything about the two people he kidnapped?"

"I wished I could help you guys! I mind my own business around here."

Says uncooperative Jim,

One man at the pool table getting ready to shoot for the eight ball overhears and responds.

"The Americans took him out of here months ago. Then he escaped to China. He must be … loving those Chinese women. Try Beijing!"

Rude Buay and Tate head out to their vehicle. They wait and survey.

Rude Buay notifies his other agents in the accompanying minivan through the stereo system.

"Nothing there, everyone is so tight lipped. Except for one drunk who said he's in Beijing."

Hudson asks,

"So what do we do?"

Rude Buay responds,

"We will persist until we find him. Even if he is under a rock we will scratch him out like… crayfish.

Hudson responds,

"I've never been to China before. I am all in!"

Tate looks over at Rude Buay and asks,

"Is that the same as shrimp?"

Rude Buay answers,

"Close!"

Tate continues,

"You did say China? You think Ortiz would Green-light such an expedition? Why aren't these locals leading us to him?"

Rude Buay responds,

"In West Kingston, no one trusts anyone. Johnny is like a politician. He has been so good to those people; no one wants to bring him down."

Tate responds,

"But he is wanted. Why don't they?"

"He performs his dirty work. Then treats them like a modern day Santa Claus would. He has learned a lot from Alberto in that regard...."

Rude Buay says.

Banks and Heidi Hudson overhear this conversation between Rude Buay and agent Tate as broadcast through the van's stereo.

During this interlude, two local men fully armed, come up towards Banks' minivan and addresses Banks.

Banks rolls down the window to hear them.

"Got to move these supped up minivans, can't park them out here."

They both focus in on Heidi Hudson. Rude Buay and Tate are alerted, and are poised to assist if necessary.

"Is that your pimp...?"
One of the men asks,
Hudson acts as if she isn't sure what he's talking about.
Looking at Banks they continue,
"If he is pimp daddy I would like to..."
One of the men grabs on Hudson's arm, while aiming his gun on Banks.
Hudson blasts the gun carrying man who falls dead onto the street. Before the other man could release Hudson's arm and reach for his gun, Banks caps him in the head. He falls onto the street a dead man. Meanwhile Rude Buay and Tate stand erect and ready to unleash. Both agents return their guns in holster and hop inside the minivan.
Banks and Hudson board the other minivan and drive off.

22

The following morning, the agents continue combing through West Kingston for the hostages.

Hudson notices a gathering as they cross an intersection. She notifies Rude Buay through the stereo system.

"Rude Buay, pull over, these kids are way too young..."

Banks parks and Hudson rushes out leaving the door ajar.

Rude Buay complies.

Rude Buay's vehicle makes a quick U-Turn. Heidi Hudson is already out of the car in pursuit of the teenage crowd. Now the other three agents are on foot heading in agent Hudson's direction.

Agent Hudson is catching up to a 14 - 15 year old Afro-Asian girl, Tasha.

In one hand the almost subdued Tasha carries two Milky Way cans, and a switch blade in the other.

Hudson catches up with her.

She confronts Heidi Hudson.

Hudson kicks the opened knife out of Tasha's hand. Tasha rolls over on the ground. The two cans hit the pitched road and opens revealing a *Ziploc* bag with at least one eight of a kilo of cocaine underneath the powdered milk.

Banks covers Hudson, while Tate confiscates the narcotics.

Rude Buay looks on.

Agent Hudson addresses Tasha:

"What is your name young lady?"

"Tasha Ching,"

"How old are you?"

"I am almost 15,"

"Why aren't you in school?"

"Please don't tell my parents, they will kill me."

"How long have you been doing this?"

"One and a half years,"

'Why"

"The money is good,"

"How did you get involved?"

"Johnny introduced me on my 13th birthday. He said I would get rich doing the streets like him,"

"What is your address?"

"I don't have one,"

"Where do your parents live?"

"I can't tell you."

Rude Buay walks over into Tasha's space.

"Tasha, my name is agent Bascombe, some people call me Rude Buay.

"You mean like in Rihanna's song?"

Tasha immediately begins to sing and dance to the hit song by *Rihanna*.

Come here rude boy,
 boy Can you get it up Come here rude boy,
boy Is you big enough Take it,
take it Baby, baby Take it,
take it Love me, love me.
Tonight I'mma let you be the captain
Tonight I'mma let you do your thing,
yeah Tonight I'mma let you be a rider
Giddy up
Giddy up
Giddy up, babe

"The name is the same. We are here to help you and will handle this intelligently."

"You don't know my parents, they will KILL me."

Hudson interjects,

"We will ask them not to."

"I don't know why you all want to help me I am nobody..."

Rude Buay interrupts,

"That' what society makes you think. You are filled with potential, Tasha."

"My parents are not together,"

Hudson questions,

"You live at home, mom?"

"Yes,"

Tasha replies,

"Where is Johnny now?"

Rude Buay asks,

"I have not seen *Too Bad* in almost a week. They said that he went to China."

Tasha says,

"How did you get here?"

Rude Buay inquires,

"I took the bus from Kingston."

Tasha responds,

"Okay we will give you a ride,"

Says Rude Buay.

"You all promise. This is not some kind of kid-napping, right? I don't want to end up in Bermuda..."

Tasha says.

The four agents give Tasha a reassuring look.

Hudson leads the way.

Tasha follows Hudson and boards the gray minivan. The two minivans take off. The gray van leads the way towards Kingston.

23

The agents arrive in Kingston. Tasha points out the house on the hill inside a cul-de-sac. Both minivans pull up and park. Rude Buay and Tate get out and head up the hill towards the house. Rude Buay knocks on the door. A dark skinned Jamaican woman answers. My name is agent Bascombe, this is my partner Miles Tate. Agents Heidi Hudson and Walter Banks are inside the other van. We are here on a matter which we feel concerns you.

"The man and the woman who got kidnapped are not here, agents Bascombe and whatever your name is, Tate? And we are sure not hiding Johnny *Too Bad*."

"May we call you Miss or Mrs...?"

"You may call me Mrs. Ching. It doesn't matter he is gone. I sang him hit the road Jack. Don't come back no more... when he decide to walk out on Tasha and me."

Rude Bauy continues,

"Mrs. Ching, it is about your daughter. We found her at a location where she doesn't belong."

"Where is Tasha? I thought she said that she was going to live with her father. That..."

"We found her on the streets of West Kingston dealing narcotics."

States Rude Buay,

"I will KILL Tasha..."

Mrs. Ching responds,

Rude Buay interjects,

"That's what she told us."

Rude Buay continues,

"But we assured her that if she would cooperate by letting us bring her home, you wouldn't hurt her. Additionally, we would make sure that this is handled intelligently."

"Where is Tasha?"

Agent Heidi Hudson, overhearing the conversation via the "wired" Rude Buay, with Banks and Tasha listening in, steps out of the gray minivan and hands over Tasha to her mother."

"Thank you very much agents, Hudson, Bascombe, Tate and will you let Mr. Banks know that I say thanks. Is he the one who escaped getting kidnapped?"

Banks steps out of the minivan to deliver Tasha's forgotten sweater.

Mrs. Ching gets a closer view of the Jamaican agent Walter Banks.

"I am sure I heard about him on the news last week. Yes that's him. You all be careful now. It is like a jungle out there..."

Tears well-up in Tasha's eyes.

"Thanks and goodbye."

Tasha says.

The agents depart.

24

Meanwhile in Shanghai, China a submarine surfaces at an abandoned dock. There are no on-lookers, so the five individuals get off undetected: Denise, Shelly, Amanda and Johnny *Too Bad*, and a blindfolded woman. They escort the blindfolded to a waiting van, seats her inside, the van takes off with David Lee at the driver's wheel.

The van pulls up outside the *Torture House*. They exit and remove the previously blindfolded Mildred from her seat and amble towards the interior of the house.

The move descends to the desolate basement. Nothing there except for the four walls a chair in the middle of the room and a noose from a rope dangling from the extended roof. With her mouth still covered with duct tape, Shelly removes the blindfold which clothed Mildred's eyes. On Mildred's face there is a sense of frustration of wanting to speak and not being able to.

The three women bind Mildred's hand as well as her feet to the chair with ropes. Johnny overseeing grabs the slow moving extended noose and slips it around Mildred's neck. He adjusts the chair downwards, so the rope around her neck tightens just a bit.

They feel satisfied with the proper functioning of their mechanism. They depart and board the waiting van. The van drives off.

Rude Buay checks in with the Chinese immigration authorities but they are unable to verify that Johnny along with other members of the Dragon Drug Cartel had entered the country.

MEANWHILE, VULTURES FLY LOW over a small reservation, as the morning sun begins to cast its rays on the outskirts of Tivoli Gardens. In the interim, in TG, Rude Buay, Miles Tate, Heidi Hudson and Walter Banks continue their search for the kidnapped. Even so, they are still uninformed regarding Mildred's whereabouts.

The four agents continue to comb through huts, houses, tenement yards, bars along with other buildings. They are now joined by Jamaican police in the search with dogs.

Rude Buay pulls up at a Barber Shop. He gets out of his car followed by Tate.

In the meantime, Hudson and Banks visit the restaurant across the street.

Inside the barber shop: Some men are getting their hair cut, while others wait their turn.

Rude Buay, surveys, and then addresses: "My name is agent Bascombe and this is agent Tate. We are with the Drug Enforcement Agency. We are looking for Johnny *Too Bad* along with the kidnapped Mildred Simms and Baptiste."

FRITZ, who is baldheaded and certainly not there to get a haircut says nonchalantly,

"We heard about you Rude Buay! You have bigger issues in America, like Child Care, Recession and Abortion. I hope that the Prime Minister of Jamaica isn't paying you out of our hard earned tax dollars. That man Baptiste deserves to get what he received. The woman Simms, her past is what got her in trouble. Nobody in Tivoli Gardens is going to help you, *mon*. You came to the wrong place."

Rude Buay continues,

"Has anyone seen any of the hostages or know of their whereabouts?"

Everyone is mute.

"And for you sir,"

Rude Buay looks directly at the "smart mouth" local.
"Empty all your pockets and place the contents on this table."
Fritz hesitates in fulfilling agent Rude Buays' request, and finds himself suddenly looking down the barrels of two guns, Rude Buays' and Tates' semi-automatics. Out of his pockets come a switch blade knife, vials of crack and packets of cocaine.
Tate immediately cuffs him and waits for the Jamaican police to arrive in their squad car and take him away. Two officers who previously abandoned the search return and take Fritz to jail.
In the meantime, at a restaurant across the street, Hudson confronts the MANAGER on Duty.
Heidi Hudson addresses,
"Good morning! My name is agent Hudson. I am looking for Johnny *Too Bad*. Have you seen him lately? Or heard about the whereabouts regarding the kidnapped Simms and Baptiste?"
The Manager serving beef patty and cocoa bread to a customer responds,
"Fire!"
Hudson asks,
"What do you mean?"
The woman reiterates in *patois*,
"Fire ah go burn them. Them hurt poor Johnny's feelings."
Banks responds,

"Does he really have feelings?"
Leaving that for the woman to massage and marinate
Banks and Hudson unfortunately leave the Jamaican
restaurant unaccomplished.

25

Rude Buays' phone rings. He answers it on the second ring.
"Hello agent Rude Buay,"
The female voice echoes,
"This is Christine the Commissioners' wife. Has there been any word yet on Richard's whereabouts? If no ransom has been requested as of now, the chances of him still being alive are pretty slim, don't you think? It been a few days now."

"Mrs. Baptiste we are doing everything possible to try and locate your husband Richard, as well as his kidnappers.

Our hope is that we'll find Richard alive. So far I hate to inform you but nothing has turned up positively except that the Jamaican police, a short while ago claimed that they were able to trace the FedEx package which was sent to your home as being sent from Tivoli Gardens.

However, as you had seen on that package, the sender's name was ineligible. I am very optimistic that we'll find him. We will notify you as soon as we locate your husband."

Christine hears agent Rude Buay but doesn't believe anyone at this point. In tears Christine continues, this time talking to herself.

"I don't know what they want my husband for. Whatever political party gave power to this drug cartel, is putting our country to shame. We used to be one love, now it seems like one hate. Innocent people, including kids die for nothing. Who gave drug dealers power over civilians? The government and their MPs! Richard always believed in ONE Jamaica. Now the same team he assembled in order to protect and serve. They all are sitting on their butts, so vultures can devour his body and ants his bones. The country he has worked so hard to defend, has allowed the oppressors to continually oppress...Like Bob Marley said: 'Who the cap fit wear it.'

Those wicked politicians! No one is going to get my vote again."

Christine aborts her call to agent Rude Buay.

Suddenly her house phone rings. She tries catching it on the second ring, misses it but grabs it on the third.

"Hello, Hello, Hello!"

Christine addresses.

There is no answer.

The only sound she hears is "Click. Click"

Terrified, Christine bolsters herself and rushes to the bedroom. She removes one of the pillows and pulls out her husband's automatic weapon. She checks to make sure that it's loaded. Satisfied, she sits on the couch facing the door and waits.

Up the street, oblivious to her, and out of view by her property's surveillance cameras, two Jamaican police officers hideout.

These watchers, dispatched earlier after the tracking location of FedEx package was determined by a Government Official and ally of Johnny and Alberto Gomez, continue to wait.

Already tapped into Christine's phone line they gather information.

On their TV monitor the police could see Christine waiting for the kill.

It's dawn. The policemen look at each other, none of them dare becoming a casualty, so they unwillingly vacate the area.

26

B ack in Tivoli Gardens, Rude Buay not giving up continues to follow his instincts. Driving further along Mannings Hill they come up on a blockage in the street. The blockade made up of abandoned ice boxes, car tires, tree trunks, bed mattresses, old furniture, tree branches, skeleton of stripped vehicles and oil drums. Rude Buay, Miles Tate, Walter Banks and Heidi Hudson get out of their vehicle and make a clear path. They re-board their vehicle and proceed along the same street.

At an undisclosed location in Tivoli Gardens, Alberto reclines the black leather chair and sip on the almost full cup of that black robust coffee. He reaches for his phone and dials.

Rude Buay and his agents continue combing the streets looking for any evidence which could lead them to the finding of the hostages.

Rude Buays' cell phone rings, he answers:

"This is Rude Buay."

Rude Buay realizes its Alberto Gomez's number and goes to full circuit stereo. The two agents in the other minivan listen in. The voice on the other end greets.

"Rude Buay, this is Albert Gomez. It is apparent that you and your agents will not take a back seat by letting me do my thing as I see fit. First I must inform you that the man you are looking for is sitting under my thumb. And very soon you could be accompanying him if you continue to be in pursuit of my enterprise. Don't forget we not only control Tivoli Gardens, We are global..."

Rude Buay interrupts:

"All that you are saying is old news. Understand that every seed you've planted has the ability to sprout but that doesn't mean that it will. I am interested in the two hostages, not what you and David Lee has put together globally."

"That won't happen unless you and your agents are willing to comply with our demands."

Alberto says,

"Try me!"

Rude Buay answers courageously.

"You failed at living up to demands back in Port Antonio. Not sure you are capable of keeping your word."

States Alberto.

"You are nothing but a prick!"

Rude Buay responds.

"You have one hour to withdraw your antagonistic pursuits of the Dragon Cartel. I have a private jet waiting at a hanger outside the Kingston airport and a van, plus a motorcade waiting to escort you to it if you so desire. After you and your peeps clear Jamaican airspace en-route to America, I would be happy to release Simms and the Commissioner, one at a time."

"Why are you doing this? If you have gotten your wish, why drip on the releasing process of the hostages?"

Alberto continues,

"You don't ask questions at this point Rude Buay, you fulfill demands. That's the way I choose to lay my safety net. Additionally, I am sending a message to Washington, that if they mess with us any further we will not only expand across the five oceans but will cause some of the most devastating recalls that country has ever experienced."

Alberto continues,

"As for you? If you screw up, vultures would enjoy fresh meat of you and your agents."

Rude Buay weighs the consequences and asks,

"Where is that van located?"

"You are thinking on your feet."

Alberto's coffee cup is refilled by a tall Jamaican woman. His UZI is present and close to his reach. Money and milk cans create a decorative aurora of drug dealing spectacle. Alberto snorts two lines of coke, one per nostril. Alberto fetches his gun and car keys. He leaves. Even so, he continues his phone conversation with Rude Buay.

Alberto continues,

"It's located at the entrance of Tivoli Gardens, on the Southwest corner."

BACK AT THE ENTRANCE TO TG, the van waits, along with a pair of motor bikes and two men standing guard.

ON ANOTHER TIVOLI GARDENS STREET, the agents park their cars.

Rude Buay puts Alberto on hold and commissions his other agents via the stereo.

"Banks and Hudson I need you to cover on the outside of this property while Tate and I engage on this investigative pursuit."

Rude Buay releases the hold button and continues his conversation with Alberto.

Rude Buay replies,

"Alberto it's a deal. How soon will we be able to take custody of Baptiste and Simms?"

Alberto responds,

"They belong to the Jamaican Government. You have my word that they will be released simultaneously to their government."

Rude Buay not believing a word Alberto says.

Alberto continues,

"Good! That private jet flies in 48 minutes."

The agents continue their search of West Kingston. After driving through most of TG, Rude Buay sees a house with an outdoor sign saying "beware of dogs." He pulls over. Banks does vice versa. Alberto's guards are unaware of the agents' entourage forming outside the front door.

Upon noticing the black and gray vans parked outside the house. The guards release a few rounds from Uzis in the vehicles direction.

The vans are empty as the four agents had already dispersed and taken up position on the other side of the house. One of the guards fires at Rude Buay. He misses and takes a bullet from Rude Buays' gun instead. That guard hits the ground, dead.

27

Heidi Hudson enters the house through the already opened front door amidst the sound of barking dogs. The tall Jamaican woman attempts to escape. The agile Heidi Hudson pushes her back inside with vengeance.

Heidi Hudson asks,

"Where are Simms and Baptiste?"

The Woman does not respond. So Hudson handcuffs her.

"You are going with us."

Says Hudson as she pushes the woman in-front of her like a human shield proceeding through the house's interior.

In the interim, Rude Buay and Tate are still engaged in an exchange of fire power with the other guard. Rude Buay shoots. The Guard runs for the parked car. A bullet catches the guard disconnected and cuts him down.

MEANWHILE, OBLIVIOUS TO the agents, Alberto boards a waiting submarine from an abandoned dock in Kingston.

Back at the House in Tivoli Gardens, Rude Buay, Tate and Banks catch up with Heidi Hudson as they penetrate deep inside the interior of that house. Rude Buay observes the handcuffed woman. Like a man possessed he asks,

"Where are Baptiste and Simms?"

The woman now hearing this asked of her by two separate agents. Yet, she still refuses to cooperate.

Inside the living room, money and milk cans create a decorative and auroras drug dealing spectacle.

The agents move deeper inside the interior of the strange house. Walter Banks is already leading the way followed by Rude Buay, Tate, Hudson and the Jamaican Woman.

The barking sounds of multiple dogs alert the agents to open a locked door. Rude Buay blows out the lock with a bullet from his gun.

As they enter in take-down style, three chained blood hounds forming a periphery plunge in desperation towards them.

The starving, chained dogs intermittently salivate at their prey that is chained to an electric wired chair. Bones and blood residue add to the presence of recent carnivorous activities.

When the dogs plunge fully forward the extent of the chains, place their mouths at least three feet in-front of the chained victim.

Walter Banks recognizes the victim and yells out,

"It's the Commish!"

Rude Buay advises,

"Let's get him out of here swiftly."

Four guns are pointed on the three dogs. As the agents get ready to take the drooling dogs out of their misery, the Jamaican Woman yells,

"Cease fire!"

The animals lock eyes with the Jamaican Woman and retreat. Not leaving anything up to chance, the agents maintain their aim on the three blood hounds. Heidi Hudson sizes up the situation.

"I got it!"

Hudson marches in the midst of that "dog's den." She notices the Commissioner wired to the max.

Walter Banks senses trouble and says,

"Be care-ful Hudson, I hear a ticking sound. Any wire you touch could send us all up in smoke."

Banks gets on his cell phone and dials Chelo in Bogota, Colombia.

Chelo is fast asleep. He jumps up and grabs the phone.

"Chelo! I am sleeping."

Says Chelo,

"Wake up man we are under a time crunch. Need your help. We found the Commissioner. He is wired to the max, multiple red blue and black wires."

Relays Walter Banks,

Chelo asks,

"What is the address?"

Banks replies,

"No address, a great big house in Tivoli Gardens off Mannings Hill. Come on Chelo, give us your best shot."

Chelo fumbles around with various monitor screens. He claims,

"I got it! Wait."

Ticking decibels increase.

Heidi Hudson responds,

"There is no… time to wait, we could all get killed."

Chelo replies,

"Banks, tell Hudson not to touch anything on that man not even his clothing. The only way out is to turn off the power switch located at the circuit breaker."

Banks looks over at the Jamaican woman and asks,

"Where is the darn circuit breaker?"

The Jamaican Woman reluctantly points towards an adjacent room across the hall.

Chelo assures,

"She is right! Move quickly. Time is running out!"

Rude Buay pulls out another automatic from under his trousers. He points it on the dogs where Banks' aim was directed.

Banks tugs the woman to that room where she indicated the power turn-off switch is.

In the interim the dogs plunge forward at Agent Hudson with the full length of their chain.

Tate yells,

"Cease fire!"

There is no response from the dogs. Rude Buay and Hudson follow up using the same command to no avail.

Total darkness now engulfs the room, mixed with sounds of barking dogs and the mumbling of the agents.

Banks and the woman return with the aid of his mini-emergency flash-light.

The Jamaican woman again yells,

"Cease Fire!"

The dogs retreat. With the aid of Banks' flash light, he and Hudson remove the Commissioner, who is still wearing the clothes he did when kidnapped. Together the agents make their getaway from inside the house.

Rude Buay asks the woman,

"Any information on Mildred Simms whereabouts?"

The Jamaican woman replies,

"Try Shanghai."

As the agents make their exit on the house's terrace, Banks pulls out five U.S one hundred dollar bills, and attempts to hand it over to the woman, who is still handcuffed.

Hudson grabs the cash and sticks it inside of the woman's bra. Meanwhile, the agents quickly remove the duct tape from the Commissioners' mouth.

The Commissioner now vocal,

Thank you Mr. Rude Buay and...

Rude Buay assists,

Tate, My partner Miles Tate.

The Commissioner,

"Tate. Tis so great seeing all you good people once again. I missed the de-briefing. Thanks Hudson, great intuition. Banks we appreciate you!"

Rude Buay states,

"No problem we got you out of there safely. Now we've got to go and find Mildred Simms."

The Commissioner asks,

"Where is Mildred? They got her too?"

Rude Buay expounds,

"Yes. Also kidnapped by the Dragons on the same evening as you ..."

They load up, place the Commissioner inside the gray minivan and depart from the premises, leaving the woman behind still in handcuffs.

28

It's nightfall. At the Tivoli Gardens entrance, the cube van waits. The agents get ready to board. A RASTAFARIAN GUARD accompanied by the driver ushers in Rude Buay and his crew.

The Rastafarian Guard says to the driver.

"Overload!"

Driver asks,

"What you mean overload?"

The Rastafarian Guard answers in deep *patois*,

"Me say overload, one too many *mon*."

The Driver and Guard stare at the Commissioner, who is bearded and outfitted in street clothes, wearing a Rastafarian wig and dark sun glasses. His fashionable tie is hanging out from his side pocket.

Rude Buay argues,

"We've got to take him or we don't go."

The driver continues staring at the Rastafarian Guard and Baptiste.

The Rastafarian Guard responds,

"That man is not getting inside this van. I was told four people now five show up. Not another thug!"

The driver and the guard continue arguing, creating a stand-off against the agents and the Commissioner. The Guard senses trouble not knowing what to expect at this point from the agents. So he commands,

"Drop your weapons!"

The agents comply.

While the Guard moves the four guns to the side and out of the way. Rude Buay kicks him hard in the stomach. The Guard falls to the ground gasping for air. The Guard quickly regains his presence of mind. He aims at Rude Buay and shoots.

Rude Buay dodges out of his onslaught and reaches for the gun under his left trousers leg. He gets a successful shot off, which caps the Rastafarian Guard. The driver swings at Rude Buay. His swing is blocked by Rude Buay using his left hand and his right hand to punch him hard in his face, as a result, knocking him out.

The four agents and the Commissioner swiftly load up ammunition and luggage from the minivans onto the cube van. They board the van. The Commissioner, under Rude Buays' instruction, takes the wheel.

The van departs through the streets of Kingston. Suddenly, Rude Buays' phone rings. He answers.

"My pilot flies in ten minutes."

Says Alberto.

"Blame it on your drivers."

Rude Buay responds.

"We'll make it anyway."

Rude Buay continues and then hangs up.

Later they arrive at the airport hangar in Kingston. The Cube van pulls up next to the waiting Jet aircraft. They disembark and come face to face with the Pilot and his co-pilot.

The Pilot's eyes are focused on the Commissioner. Something doesn't seem right to him. Looking at Rude Buay he says,

"You are late Rude Buay, this plane should have flown five minutes ago, David Lee wouldn't be very happy with this."

Says the Pilot.

Richard Baptiste, the Commissioner responding to the name drop, asks.

"I thought it was ... Alberto?"

The Pilot answers as a matter of fact,

"On his way to … Asia! Got to move it …!"

Looking over at the Co-Pilot, the Pilot instructs,

"Frisk them down and get those bastards on board."

The Co-Pilot complies.

They are clean except for Rude Buay still carrying that gun in his left trousers' leg.

The Pilot takes away Rude Buay's gun, removes the bullets and tosses it away.

The Commissioner attempts getting on the Jet last.

The Pilot is alerted.

"We are not taking you. Trying to get into America illegally?"

He continues,

"Not going to happen. Plus we don't have an extra seat anyway. You could ride on the wing."

Says the Pilot.

In protest the four agents deplane headed by Rude Buay. The Pilot is confused. He commands.

"Get your asses back on that plane. I'll take you to Miami dead or alive. It's your choice."

He aims his gun at them.

The Co-Pilot's back is turned against the aircraft. Rude Buay grabs him behind his neck, lifts him off the ground while his feet dangles. He drops him hard to the ground, takes away his weapon, caps him several times and then aims gun at the pilot.

The Pilot has a change of heart.

"It's okay we will take your friend if that's what you want."
Rude Buay commands,
"Drop your weapons!"
The Pilot is flustered but he complies.
Tate and Banks check the Pilot for additional weapons. There is none.
Rude Buay shoves the Pilot aboard the Jet and commands,
"Open up the hatch."
The Pilot does as commanded.
Rude Buay keeps an aim on the pilot, while the Commissioner and the other agents load up their weapons and luggage onto the aircraft.
Everyone is now on board.
Pilot sits at the control of the Jet.
Rude Buay announces,
"Change of plans! We are going to Shanghai, China."
The Pilot remarks,
"Never been there before. Navigation could be problematic. Plus I don't speak their language."
Rude Buay weighs his options.
Richard Baptiste gets up from his seat,
"Don't worry I got this! I've taken off and landed in Shanghai on numerous occasions."
The pilot gets up, relinquishing control to Baptiste.
Rude Buay grabs the pilot and pushes him through the door and off the plane.

He tries to get away on foot. Several rounds from Rude Buays' gun cuts him down as he collapses to his death.

The plane taxis and then takes off.

29

It's a crisp busy morning. The hustle and bustle of the white collar workforce resembles that of New York's Wall Street, prior to the sound of the big bell and the Wall Street protests of 2011. Retrospectively, across the way an African American freestyler draws a crowd of Asian supporters like a vacuum in motion. Chu Ling joins the mesmerized audience.

Up the block, two Chinese Police Officers converse, while looking in the direction of the crowd. Their eyes are now fixed on Chu, who seems to be mesmerized by the artistic performance. The officers proceed toward the gathering and confront Chu Ling.

The senior Chinese police officer questions,

"Miss, what are you carrying in that bag?"

Chu Ling replies,

"Groceries!"

The Junior Officer is "gun happy" while his partner continues the investigation.

The senior CHINESE POLICE OFFICER asks,

"Do you mind if we take a look?"

Chu Ling reluctantly hands over the bag.

The senior officer opens it. He sees a full container of milk nevertheless, he looks at Chu and asks as he approaches the trash can.

"If there is nothing but milk inside, we will replace it."

The senior officer pours the milk out into the trash can. A *Ziploc* bag with a powdery substance falls out on top of the milk. He retrieves it and asks,

"Miss what is your name?"

"Chu Ling."

"Chu - Ling!"

He continues,

"I am afraid this is not all milk. We are going to have to arrest you for cocaine possession."

The junior officer handcuffs Chu Ling and escorts her to their parked cruiser.

The crowd as well as the freestyler scatter as the arrest is conducted.

Moments later, on that same street, the Drug Czar David Lee meanders his way through a dense crowd of pedestrians looking for his wife Chu.

In the meantime at a prestigious law firm in downtown Shanghai, on the top floor in a high rise building twelve lawyers of the Chins Law Firm engage in their early morning free-basing ritual. Some free-base while others chip away from the cocaine mound. Others assemble and snort. Finally, they all partake. Consequently, severe vomiting and giddiness sets in later. The Law Firm's Green Room is now full with panic and pandemonium.

Less than an hour later ambulances arrive whisking all twelve lawyers to a downtown Shanghai hospital. Several blocks away the news is live on a big TV screen regarding the recent Chinese Drug Bust. People standing outside a bus station are glued to that early morning news in various languages around the world.

ONE AMERICA TV station delivers the following newscast along with footage:

"This is your early morning late breaking news from ONE AMERICA TV:"

A female American TV announcer sinks her teeth into it.

"Earlier this morning at least a dozen lawyers from Chins Law Firm in downtown Shanghai were rushed to the hospital after an apparent free-basing session. Chinese Police discovered two milk cans containing cocaine residue under the table of the office where the alleged free-basing session occurred.

Meanwhile over ten thousand cans of milk believed to have been packed with *Ziploc* bags of uncut cocaine, were discovered in a submarine down the Chinese River bound for the Caribbean. The estimated street value of the cargo is over $10M. A Colombian Drug Lord, Salvador, was arrested and detained by Chinese Police in conjunction with the drug bust.

Meanwhile, the FDA in Washington, DC has scheduled a meeting for next Monday to discuss the possibility of a recall to all powdered milk products including **baby formula**. According to analysts, if this recall goes into effect millions of kids around the world could die of scurvy and malnutrition.

Many mothers are resorting to breast feeding in an effort to protect their young ones from death or malnourished related diseases.

China, now emerging as one of the largest industrial nations is now under pressure; as anything shipped from that country is subject to search by Chinese authorities.

In addition, random searching of packages on all public transportation is now in effect in China. This morning Chinese police also arrested and detained Chu Ling, the mistress of the Drug Lord and Entrepreneur David Lee on drug trafficking charges. It is believed that Ling sold narcotics to the Chin Law firm earlier this morning."

Many mothers around the world are stunned by these latest revelations:

A mom of four kids in Utah rushes to the bedroom just to see if all her little ones under the ages of five years old were okay. She is satisfied as they are all playing with toys. She overlooks the powdered milk products on the kitchen counter and instead grabs the youngest and prepares to breast feed the infant.

One woman in Hollywood, California wishing she had kids breaks out in tears upon viewing the news.

On the other hand, one starving writer in Seattle takes copious notes with the hope that he could someday cash in on a replicated story.

30

Inside David Lee's house an intense free-basing, get high interlude unfolds around the dining table involving David Lee, Alberto Gomez, Denise Gomez, Shelly Hall, Amanda Kingsley and Johnny *Too Bad*. Johnny methodically rolls a giant sized marijuana *spliff* in the cover page of the local Chinese newspaper which covered the drug bust. He lights up, partakes and passes it off to Alberto, who takes a huge toke before passing it along to his associates.

Everyone partakes except for David Lee, who is busily separating his upcoming dosage from the huge mound of cocaine with the use of a razor blade. Then with a straw he attacks and snorts that entire line, like it was clean air.

David is now relaxed.

He addresses his associates,

"We have got to do something about Rude Buay. That jet still has not arrived in Miami."

"Orders must be carried out. Once again he reneged on..."

Responds Alberto.

Johnny interjects,

"It should be clear to him in the note from me that I want him out of TG."

Shelly chimes in,

"Out of Jamaica. Period!"

David Lee states,

"That private jet left Jamaica with two sets of casualties behind. One at the ground transportation pick-up site in Tivoli Gardens, and the other at the airplane hangar in Kingston."

Shelly reaffirms,

"Rude Buay doesn't know how to fly an airplane."

Alberto responds,

"I don't think that any of the others do ..."

Johnny interrupts,

"The Commissioner attended aviation school in China. That's where he met his wife."

Eyebrows are raised.

Johnny *Too Bad* asks,

"Boss, enough respect but how did you let that PIG get away? I thought that we had him inside the net."

Alberto responds,

"Blame it on those … guards. Too many loose ends!"

David opens his loaded wallet. He removes Chu Lings picture, and reflects. He has a moment, pondering as if in that mediatory event with his wife, she would be released from within the prison walls. Everyone in the circle up is now silent.

David Lee continues,

"Guys we need to figure out where that plane landed. There has been no communication from that pilot as of yet."

Johnny in deep thought.

Johnny *Too Bad* states,

"They took Tasha back home to her mother. I wonder if she told those bastards that I went to China."

David Lee questions,

"Who the heck is Tasha?"

Johnny *Too Bad* replies,

"She worked for me."

Amanda Kingsley is peeved.

"Risking our lives with a minor …?"

She asks.

Alberto picks up his gun and car keys off the table in preparation to depart. Getting in his way is his wife Denise.

"Where are you going to *Papi?*"

Alberto responds,

"Let's go to the airport!"

They all look at each other as if Alberto's decision was the expected magical wand needed to be waved in order to conclude the Rude Buay saga.

The get-high session escalates into a massive conclusion.

They make their exit...

31

The Jet arrives in Shanghai, China. The agents and the Commissioner deplane. With the newly acquired cell phone from Walter Banks, Baptiste dials his wife Christine for the first time after being kidnapped. Christine Baptiste answers,
"Hello, who is this?"
"This is Rich, Richard. I am free Chris! Free at last. Meet me in China. I will text you the exact location when we check in."
Christine Baptiste asks,

"WE?"

Richard Baptiste responds,

"I am with Banks, Rude Buay and the rest of their team. You remember telling me that you wanted to fly with me someday. I may consider taking up piloting … you and me Chrissie."

Christine Baptiste responds,

"Please send me your location soon. I can't wait … !"

A distinguished Asian Official dressed in white attire interrupts the celebration.

He meets and greets them at the airplane hangar. He bows in acknowledgement and points to a van in a parking spot. Rude Buay ambles towards the vehicle and looks it over.

The Official hands over the keys to Rude Buay, along with a folded piece of paper. They load up their luggage and weaponry. Rude Buay reads the address: The Lounge, 17 Chamber Lane, Shanghai.

The distinguished official looks at Rude Buay with concern.

Distinguished gentleman asks,

"Mr. Rude Buay, how is your Kung Fu?"

Rude Buay thinks it through, and replies,

"What I lack in skill I will make up in activity. And where there are no roots, sprouts will appear."

The Asian Official gives him thumbs up and smilingly departs.

The agents board the van. The Commissioner takes the wheel.

The van departs.

32

Rude Buay and his entourage arrive outside David Lee's house. Covert and desolate *The Lounge* sits on a hill. Rude Buay, Walter Banks, Heidi Hudson, Miles Tate and the Commissioner Richard Baptiste jump out. They are instantly alerted by the pacing guards on the grounds of the property, as well as the roof of that house. It's now nightfall, so Rude Buay and his men disperse and manage to surround the house. Even so, one of the patrolling guards notices the five intruders.

A patrolling guard yells out,

"We are under attack, Americans! Americans! *Jamericans!*"

Other guards jump off the roof. They emerge running through the back door as well as the front door in confrontation.

The agents all armed including the Commissioner unload several rounds of bullets on the guards.

The skilled guards retaliate and dodge out of the agent's fire power until there are no more bullets left in their guns.

Sensing their own vulnerability, one petite guard viciously approaches them Kung Fu style. No one dare take him on except for Rude Buay.

Moments later Rude Buay leaves the elfin martial artist on the ground paralyzed.

Another agent realizing the affliction rendered to his coworker comes violently at Rude Buay with the "crane" move, before Rude Buay can even compose himself. Rude Buay quickly unravels that guard and gets confronted by yet another. This agile guard quickly shows up the agents' Kung Fu deficiencies.

Witnessing, the manhandling of Rude Buay his team rushes to the parked van down the hill to acquire more bullets.

Upon returning, the guard has Rude Buay held upside down and about to smash his head on top of the paved concrete driveway.

Agent Heidi Hudson gets a shot off from her reloaded gun and shoots the guard directly in his forehead. The guard topples over, with Rude Buay falling on top of him.

Rude Buay gets up, steps on top of the guard en-route to the interior of the house with his team in tow. The other guards failing miserably to make a comeback, try fleeing past them. They all get capped by Rude Buay's team.

Rude Buay reloads his gun upon entering, thanks to the generosity of Walter Banks who supplied him with bullets.

The agents, along with the Commissioner are now inside the living room. A maid wearing an apron originates flying out of the ceiling through the man hole. Hudson sees her and instead of shooting her changes her mind and engages in hand to hand combat.

As they go at it, Hudson asks the maid,

"Where is Mildred Simms?"

Instead of getting an answer the maid engages in more Kung Fu action. Hudson hones her skill of the craft on the maid via on the job training.

In the meantime, other members of the agents' team rummage through the house.

In a room adjacent to the living room they discover: stacks of Jewish bank roll, millions of dollars in U.S. currency, Chinese currency, hundreds of *Ziploc* bags with at least one eight kilo of uncut cocaine each, American passports, grenades, survival kits, along with a massive gun collection.

Inside the next room they enter take-down style. There is no one there, but numerous milk cans arranged like on an assembly line. Rude Buay, Walter Banks, Miles Tate and The Commissioner enter another room in search of Mildred Simms. She is not there. Another room beckons, so they enter, in search of Mildred.

33

In the interim, outside the airport hangar, a convoy of cars pull up led by David Lee's BMW. Alberto's Mercedes Benz follows. Shelly, Denise and Amanda follow in their Hatchback and Johnny *Too Bad* in his Escalade. They survey for a while trying to determine if the Jet, arranged to take the agents back to Miami was flown to Shanghai instead. It's tedious as most of the jets look alike. Finally they stumble into it. Alberto opens the door and enters. The others wait outside.

Inside the cockpit of the Jet, Alberto discovers the tie Commissioner Baptiste wore at the time he was kidnapped. He alerts Johnny *Too Bad* along with his other associates. They clue in.

Shelly, Amanda and Denise take off speedily in their Hatchback. The others board their vehicle preparing to leave.

However, before the men take off a van pulls up. Four Henchmen jump out. David Lee gets out of his car with his gun aimed on the four men.

David Lee yells,

"You are late! ...Late!"

The men bow apologetically. David Lee hands a wad of dollar bills which he retrieved from his pocket along with an address on a sheet of paper. The Henchmen take off speedily. The Drug Lords take off in the opposite direction.

MEANWHILE BACK AT LEE'S HOUSE. Oblivious to Hudson's partners, agent Hudson is now confronted by Amanda Kingsley her newly arrived combat. The tired maid whimpers, bloody in the corner as a result of Hudson's spanking.

Outside Shelly and Denise wait with the car door still open after Amanda's exit.

Amanda Kingsley outdoes agent Hudson with her Kung Fu skills.

Finally Shelly yells out,

"Let's take that … to *Torture House*!

Amanda puts the agent in a choke hold and drags her outside to the waiting car.

Upon arriving, Amanda with the help of Shelly and Denise, bind Hudson with ropes, tie her hands behind her back and throw her in the back of their tinted windows vehicle.

Shelly takes the wheel. Looking in the rearview mirror she addresses agent Hudson:

"Welcome back, bitch you never learn, huh? You had your chance to be free. Stay in America with your son. Instead you are determined to mess up our livelihood."

Heidi Hudson asks,

"What do you want from me?"

Shelly responds,

"You will find out at the *Torture House*."

The car continues on its way.

Meanwhile, back inside *The Lounge*, one of Lee's other houses: the agents and the Commissioner return to the living room and notice the maid on the floor coughing up blood.

Additionally, to their surprise, they realize that agent Hudson is missing.

Looking outside, the fresh tire marks leave an imprint on the dust laden pavement. The men hustle to their vehicles to embark on a search for the missing agent Hudson.

Meanwhile, the Hatchback carrying Hudson turns the corner up the street.

Denise, never seen smoking in public before. She turns to Amanda and asks for a cigarette. Amanda grants her request. Denise lights up stating:

"I'll put that bitch out of her misery."

34

Located in the hills of Northern Shanghai on a Cul De Sac is *Torture House*. The grounds are fit for entertaining with several barbeque pits and a large swimming pool.

The three women drag Hudson inside and tie her up just like they did to the kidnapped Mildred Simms. Creating a huddle around Hudson, they continue to terrorize the agent. Shelly could have addressed any other issue to open her interrogation process of Heidi Hudson, but she chooses to go back to the last question she asked of agent Hudson during the interrogation session back in Jamaica on the previous mission.

"Who did your dad pay to take out my man in Bogota?"

Heidi Hudson responds,

"Will you just let my dad rest in peace?"

Shelly responds,

"No *Bitch*, he is not going to rest, neither are you until I find out who snuffed out Mike."

Heidi Hudson replies,

"Dad had nothing to do with your boyfriend's death."

Shelly states:

"That's what you said the last time. Your dad had every reason to hurt him. Mike decided not to split his cocaine profits with your deceptive, corrupt, deceitful dad. Therefore your dad, one of the wealthiest DEA to ever work in Miami, hired someone to kill Mike."

Heidi responds,

"I am not my father's keeper, just his daughter. You are asking me questions I can't answer."

Denise steps right into the frame. She hands over a journal to her counterpart Shelly.

Shelly removes the bookmark and begins to read silently at first.

Shelly continues,

"You wrote in your journal the day Mike was killed: 'My dad did what he had to do in order to get where he needed to go.' Did you not?"

Hudson feeling like she is being put on trial responds, "My dad was paid to do a job as a DEA. Like every loyal agent he was obligated to report the facts to his superiors. Your man was a Drug Lord and dealing drugs was, and still is, against the law."

Denise interjects,

"Is that the eleventh commandment because I never saw it in the *Ten*?"

Heidi replies,

"Everything that's wrong was not included in those two tablets of stone…"

Amanda interrupts,

"Alright Hudson enough of that Bible stuff. This is not Sunday school. Besides, my sister went way too easy on you the last time."

Amanda continues,

"May … Agnes Richards R.I.P."

Hudson reflects on the torture she encountered by Agnes and Shelly on the previous operation.

Amanda locks eyes with agent Hudson,

"FYI, I will be pushing the button for your hanging on the Sabbath. You can pray all you want. There won't be any miracle."

Amanda approaches the chair in which Hudson sits, and slaps her twice, hard in the face, and then tightens the noose hanging around the agent's neck.

The women open a closet filled with an eclectic assortment of weapons. They arm themselves to the massive.

Shelly looking back at Hudson threatens,

"We will be back! Your countdown begins right now."

BACK AT THE LOUNGE in Shanghai, Rude Buay, Miles Tate, Walter Banks and the Commissioner all race to their vehicles. Before the men could board their van, Rude Buay notices that all four van tires have been slashed as the van sits on its rims. Rude Buay kicks the tires in disgust. Thinking it through, he then advises,

"There is an option! I am going to check that parked car in the back driveway."

Rude Buay leaves the other men and departs in that direction.

He breaks inside of a parked car and tries starting it. The car does not respond so he opens the hood only to realize that the battery is missing. Rude Buay leaves searching for options.

In the meantime, a van pulls up next to the van with the slashed tires. The four Henchmen jump out. They surround Banks, Tate and Baptiste.

The three men are no match for these four henchmen. So the quartet captures the trio, strip them of all their weapons, and throw them inside their van. They jump inside the van.

The van departs up the hill, following in tow of the femme fatales.

Moments later, Rude Buay, after locating no other form of transportation, returns down the hill to the scene of that abandoned van. There is no one there. Even so, he surveys but in vain. The smell of hay and the neighing of a horse alert him to a nearby barn. He rushes to the horse shed. There he finds a horse kicking up its heels. He takes it for a ride through the village in search of Tate, Banks and Baptiste.

35

Tate, Banks and Baptiste are escorted inside an office. For the first time, they are face to face with Alberto Gomez and David Lee.

Alberto, staring at Banks states:

"Walter Banks, I knew you would show up voluntarily."

Banks pleads the fifth.

Alberto continues,

"Commissioner, you can run but you can't hide. How do you like your *Déjà Vu?*"

Alberto shoots at the Commissioner. The bullet misses his head. The Commissioner can't believe what he has been drawn into for the second time in less than a month.

Alberto looks across at his Henchmen and commands,

"Take them to the *Torture House* and leave the white guy."

The four men comply.

Tate is now on center stage in front of David Lee and Alberto Gomez.

Alberto asks,

"Agent Tate, how long have you been an agent?"

Tate responds,

"Less than one month!"

Alberto continues,

"Someone suckered you into interrupting the flow, huh? You sure handle yourself as a pro."

Tate responds,

"Thanks, I've always wanted to be a DEA. A great one!"

Alberto questions,

"How much they pay you?"

Tate answers,

"I am not really in for the money."

Alberto says,

"You are such a deceitful bastard. No wonder you always wanted to be a DEA. What are you in for, Drugs and *Hotties*?"

Tate responds,

"None of those things matter!"

David goes inside of the closet and retrieves an attaché case. He brings it out, displays it on the table in-front of agent Tate. He then opens it. Inside the attaché case: Stacks of crisp U.S. one hundred dollar bills.

Tate eyes light up.

David Lee addresses,

"Tate, we are expanding rapidly and need someone like you to head up operations at the U.S/Canadian Border. You are the right complexion and the perfect age."

David Lee hands over the attaché and encourages,

"This is a "draw."

Tate counts the money. He is excited but confused.

David Lee states,

"If you change your mind, just return the cash as is. Here is my business card."

Tate accepts the bribe.

Alberto says to Tate,

You are free to go agent Tate.

Tate departs.

Shelly, Denise, and Amanda bring in Heidi Hudson who is bruised, battered and tied up.

Alberto addresses:

"Agent Hudson, it is good to see you again. I must say that you are either stupid or Rude Buay must have brainwashed you, hypnotized you or... Is it your resilience or do you get your high from being abused?"

Hudson maintains her silence.

Alberto interrogates,

"My desire is to get you out of this situation that you have locked yourself into. You had so many opportunities to be free. Yet, you won't leave the DEA business. It seems like you are trying to cash in, like your dad."

David goes to the closet and returns with an attaché case. He opens it on the table in-front of agent Hudson. The case is stacked with U.S. one hundred dollar bills.

David Lee argues,

"Agent Hudson here is what we can do for you. We are expanding and need your expertise at the Nogales border in Arizona. You fit the profile of who we are looking for to head up that operation. We don't want to use one of *us* just not yet."

Agent Hudson stares at the loot.

"No thanks, I will not be bribed."

Says Hudson.

Alberto continues,

"Agent are you sure you want to pass this up with bonuses and incentives added? We would be also willing to bury the hatchet - your dad's."

Alberto looks across at Shelly Hall for validation.

Heidi Hudson reiterates,

"I am not interested even if it cost me my life."

Alberto looking across at Shelly.

"Take her back to the *Torture House*! We'll hang her tomorrow."

Denise asks,

"What do we do with Mildred Simms?"

Alberto responds,

"Leave her for Johnny, along with Banks and Baptiste. He wants them for Jamaica. Bring us Rude Buay alive. Hudson?... We'll hang her ass tomorrow."

36

The three female Drug Lords, Shelly, Denise and Amanda rough up agent Hudson excessively as they take her to their car. They push her inside and drive off back to the *Torture House.*

In the meantime, Rude Buay continues riding briskly through the villages of northern Shanghai; in search of the other members of his team. He dials Banks, Baptiste, Hudson and Tate in succession. There is no response from any of them. So he dials Chelo, and gets a busy tone.

Back in Bogota, Chelo is on the roof top busy rewiring his equipment, and misses that call.

Rude Buay hangs up and redials as the horse gallops along the narrow streets of the village. Still no one picks up his call. From the streets he can see Chinese kids playing at the park. The kids are now focused on him. Somewhat thrilled to see a man riding on a horse through their neighborhood.

One kid yells out,

"Holy Grail! Holy Grail!"

Finally, Chelo aborts the rooftop equipment renovation and re-enters his shack. He notices the blinking light and responds to the missed call.

Rude Buay picks up.

"Rude Buay, I have been working all day on the roof installing a new antenna, *señor*. Now I have new video for you."

Rude Buay replies,

"I am not in a vehicle right now, Chelo. You are going to have to describe those visuals for me."

Chelo asks,

"What is your location, agent Rude Buay?"

Rude Buay responds,

"On a horse Chelo, in northern Shanghai, give me what you got Chelo."

Chelo replies,

"I have some recent footage from inside a building known as the *Torture House*. Shelly, Denise and

Amanda were viewed terrorizing agent Hudson. Walter Banks, the Commissioner and Mildred Simms and Hudson are all possibly awaiting their hanging. I was able to track Johnny *Too Bad*. He just left the dock and boarded a taxi. He could be heading to the hanging or pursuing you."

"Where is that house Chelo?"

"In a *Cul De Sac* in Northern Shanghai, no address listed. That is a very remote location."

Says Chelo.

"Thanks. Anything on agent Tate?"

"Nothing, Zip, *Nada*. He could have been kidnapped, and sent to a different location or already killed by the Dragon Cartel."

Rude Buay responds,

"Thanks Chelo ..."

Rude Buay hurries through the remote village. His phone rings, he gets it.

"Rude Buay, Johnny just made a stop a mile east of your location at a place called the *Wood House*. It is situated one mile north of your location. Looks like he's about to make a deal..."

Chelo advises.

Rude Buay challenges the horse to speed up and proceeds riding in that direction.

37

RUDE BUAY pulls up on the horse outside the *Wood House*. The street is swamped with expensive automobiles. He enters the house armed in search of the DRAGONS. Johnny makes a transfer of cash with two drug dealers earlier, who now leave, oblivious to the agent. Johnny proceeds towards the door with the attaché case filled with money. He unexpectedly runs into Rude Buay waiting for him on his way inside the house.

Johnny shoots at Rude Buay and darts back inside the office where that transaction was made earlier.

Johnny's bodyguards are alerted. Rude Buay pursues and is confronted by Johnny's body guard.

In the interim, Johnny loads two guns, and sticks them in his waist. While additional BODYGUARDS hurry to the roof top and position for battle.

Rude Buay, in *Terminator* style eliminates the first body-guard.

There's movement on top of the building. The fast paced footsteps on the roof, alerts Rude Buay that he is about to be cornered and possibly terminated by such an entourage.

Johnny emerges from the office. He opens fire on Rude Buay. Rude Buay eludes Johnny's onslaught and makes his way to the roof of the building to gain an advantage.

Rude Buay confronts one of the roof top bodyguards. They engage in a massive shoot out at each other.

The bodyguard searches for a perfect aim, and settles after succeeding. Yet, he misses as Rude Buay dodges out of it. Rude Buay finally gains the upper hand when he caps the bodyguard between both eyes.

Suddenly, Johnny emerges on the rooftop. Just before Rude Buay fires, a hail of bullets rain from Johnny's gun and ricochet from behind the wall protecting Rude Buay.

In the heat of battle Rude Buay shoots several rounds in the direction where the bullets came from and hits Johnny *Too Bad* in his right upper arm. Johnny's gun, previously in his right hand falls to the ground. Johnny *Too Bad* quickly engages in continued attack on Rude Buay using the gun in his left hand. He fires off several rounds. However, nothing connects. The gun is now empty, unknown to Rude Buay.

"Come, Johnny *Too Bad*. Show me what you've got." Rude Buay says,

"I and I rule, Rude Buay. You should know that by now." Says Johnny in *Patois*.

While shooting with the left hand, Johnny kneels down and retrieves the fallen gun.

Meanwhile, Rude Buay reloads his empty guns amidst the dodging of bullets.

Johnny is now holding two guns once again, but shoots using the gun in his right hand. Rude Buay clues in. Rude Buay continues shooting at him.

Finally, Johnny's gun is empty. Rude Buay senses Johnny's vulnerability and shoots Johnny in the forehead. Johnny falls off the building and onto the ground two stories below. Rude Buay retrieves the note from his breast pocket. It reads:

Rude Buay,

You should know by now that I and I rule. Every week at least one PIG gets killed. If you don't leave Tivoli Gardens, we would have to add you to that quota.

J.T.B.

Rude Buay folds it many times creating a paper airplane. He later shoots it in the direction of Johnny's corpse. The object falls on top of Johnny's body.

At the same time, back at the *Torture House*, Shelly, Denise and Amanda continually terrorizes agent Hudson. Upon learning of Johnny's death though, the three women rush to their Hatchback and depart speedily towards the *Wood House*. They notice Johnny's body in the street.

"I will take on Rude Buay." Says Denise.

"This is my turn, Shelly. You faced off with him last time." Amanda says,

"I have a spanking for his ..." She continues.

Rude Buay comes down to the ground level of the *Wood House*. The three women confront him. Realizing that his gun is out of bullets, Amanda decides that she will take him on in hand to hand combat. She envisions taking Rude Buay alive after the serious spanking she's about to give him.

"Go girl! Show him what you got!"

Shelly and Denise yell out to their female counterpart. Shelly's phone rings displaying the number from the *Torture House*.

Sensing that Amanda has the upper hand, and not aware that agent Rude Buay has honed his martial arts skills they depart, leaving Amanda to humiliate agent Rude Buay. They hustle back to attend to business at the *Torture House*.

38

Inside the *Torture House*, Heidi Hudson wrestles with the rope that binds her hands and feet. Using her teeth she gnaws away at the remaining strands. Finally, she manages to break herself free. She hustles over to the next room where Mildred Simms is tied up on a chair. She sets Mildred free, and together they try making their getaway.

In a room on their way out, agent Hudson notices Walter Banks and the Commissioner also tied up. Even so, Banks has managed to move his chair close to a pillar. With his left shoe he managed to sever the land line.

Mildred notices something: three guns on the table. She grabs two and Hudson grabs the other.

Suddenly, the garage door opens. The Hatchback carrying Shelly and Denise pull into the driveway and parks there instead.

Inside the house, Mildred frees Walter Banks, while agent Hudson frees the Commissioner. All four of them exit the building in haste through the side door, passing by the four dangling nooses.

Shelly and Denise are now inside the house, entering through the back door next to the pool. They miss the quartet.

Heidi Hudson shoots at the multi propane tanks in the Barbecue pit. While Mildred blows up the Hatchback with several rounds. The house goes up in flames progressively.

Back at the *Wood House* Rude Buay and Amanda are still going at each other, Kung Fu style. Amanda is putting a whopping on Rude Buay, she is taking him to *101* Kung Fu school. Just when it seems like her vision is close to becoming reality, the sound of a speeding vehicle summons.

On the outside, David Lee is racing in his BMW towards the SCENE. His car pulls up outside. He darts out and heads to the interior of the *Wood House*.

David Lee notices as Rude Buay sends Amanda to the ground with a flying kick to her upper rib-cage.

Wasting no time, David Lee sees this as an opportunity to capture Rude Buay. So he joins in for a possible two on one takedown of the agent. Though, before he can make a go at Rude Buay. Amanda gets back up but succumbs to a broken neck by another kick from the agent, landing her on the ground. This infuriates David Lee as he attacks Rude Buay with a vengeance. His first kick sends Rude Buay flying. The agent artfully lands on his feet like a cat falling on all fours.

David Lee continues his flying kick tirade on Rude Buay. The agent shows signs of exhaustion like a boxer resting against the ropes. There is no bell so the duel continues anyway.

There is a sudden crash, and like the effects of an earthquake, the building rocks back and forth. The cube truck fully loaded with cans of milk, and driven by Alberto Gomez slams into one of the main pillars supporting the *Wood House*.

Finally, the truck comes to a complete stop. As a result, not only is the *Wood House* lodging the penetrated truck but David Lee's attention gets diverted by the crash.

Rude Buay seizes the opportunity and lands a variation of flying kicks and jabs into David Lee's body. One kick strikes David Lee in his groin area.

The drug czar is shaken up and hobbles to the corner foaming through his mouth.

Rude Buay, not letting up comes at him again with an arsenal of hits. The final of which puts David Lee's head into a fix. The drug czar falls over with a broken neck.

Rude Buay, not taking any chances delivers a series of kicks into David Lee's stomach, finishing him off.

Alberto Gomez hurries out of the wreckage and center stage, just in time to witness the demolishment of his associate David Lee. He is peeved. Not sure if he should confront the agent in hand to hand combat, he resorts to shooting at Rude Buay although he would rather take him alive.

CLICK! CLICK! CLICK!

Alberto realizes that Rude Buay's gun is now empty. So he takes him on in hand to hand combat.

The brawl ensues as Rude Buay lands on top of him and knocking Alberto Gomez to the ground. The two men go at it for a while attempting to punch each other's daylights out.

The exhausted Rude Buay begins attacking Alberto with a vengeance. Suddenly, there's a creaking sound as the *Wood House* begins to give way. Alberto wants Rude Buay alive but the agent is too much for him to handle, plus sensing the mayhem Alberto runs for the side door's exit.

Rude Buay is exhausted and staggers around the room chasing after Alberto. Rude Buay goes back in time.

FLASHBACK:

MILDRED KEEPS DODGING Axel James' bullets. Rude Buay with blood on his vest rolls over onto his stomach and gets a good aim at Axel. Rude Buay Discharges.

The bullet, HITS Axel right between his two eyes. He falls backward thunderously onto the deck. Niki, the 14 year old falls forward into the deep.

A mountain like wave beckons. It hits the Catamaran viciously.

Alberto, dressed in a wet suit jumps over board into the wave, unnoticed by everyone on the other ship.

The Catamaran sails speedily towards an unavoidable collapse onto the island of Cuba.

Mildred dives into the deep, and clutches Niki around her neck. Rude Buay throws out the life rope. Mildred catches it. Rude Buay reels them in.

Another mountainous wave hits the Catamaran, it slams into Cuba at full speed, bursting into flames, debris, spikes and fragments of lumber.

BACK TO PRESENT:

Entering the *Wood House* through the front door is agent Miles Tate. Rude Buay, exhausted more than ever and with blurred vision, senses a sigh of relief upon Tate's entrance.

Rude Buay yells to agent Tate,

"Shoot him! Shoot the Philistine, don't give him another chance."

Miles Tate shoots, but instead of shooting Alberto Gomez, he shoots Rude Buay. The bullet lodges in Rude Buays' upper left leg. Rude Buay falls to the ground. Simultaneously, the *Wood House* caves in on Rude Buay while agent Tate makes his escape.

Outside the *Wood House*, two vehicles race to the scene.

First the taxi pulls up, out jumps Walter Banks, Mildred Simms, agent Heidi Hudson and Richard Baptiste the Commissioner.

Right behind it a black limousine pulls up. Dr. Tamara Ross steps out, followed by the all dolled up Christine Baptiste.

Noticing the collapse, many tears are shed at the scene.

THE HORSE AUTOMATICALLY released from its post grazes on the other side of the street.

About The Author

John A. Andrews hails from the beautiful Islands of St. Vincent and the Grenadines and resides in Hollywood, California. He is best known for his gritty and twisted writing style in his National Bestselling novel - Rude Buay ... The Unstoppable. He is in (2012) releasing this chronicle in the French edition, and poised to release its sequel Rude Buay ... The Untouchable in March 2012.

Andrews moved from New York to Hollywood in 1996, to pursue his acting career. With early success, he excelled as a commercial actor. Then tragedy struck - a divorce, with Andrews granted joint custody of his three sons, Jonathan, Jefferri and Jamison, all under the age of five. That dream of becoming all he could be in the entertainment industry, now took on nightmarish qualities.

In 2002, after avoiding bankruptcy and a twisted relationship at his modeling agency, he fell in love with a 1970s classic film, which he wanted to remake. Subsequent to locating the studio which held those rights, his request was denied. As a result, Andrews decided that he was going to write his own. Not knowing how to write and failing constantly at it, he inevitably recorded his first bestseller, Rude Buay ... The Unstoppable in 2010: a drug prevention chronicle, sending a strong message to teens and adults alike

Andrews is also a visionary, and a prolific author who has etched over two dozen titles including: Dare to Make a Difference - Success 101 for Teens, The 5 Steps To Changing Your Life, Spread Some Love - Relationships 101, Quotes Unlimited, How I Wrote 8 Books in One Year, The FIVE "Ps" for Teens, Total Commitment - The Mindset of Champions, and Whose Woman Was She? - A True Hollywood Story.

In 2007, Mr. Andrews a struggling actor and author etched his first book The 5 Steps to Changing Your Life. That title having much to do with changing one's thoughts, words, actions, character and changing the world. A book which he claims shaped his life as an author with now over two dozen published titles.

Andrews followed up his debut title with Spread Some Love - Relationships 101 in 2008, a title which he later turned into a one hour docu-drama.

Additionally, during that year Andrews wrote eight titles, including: Total Commitment - The Mindset of Champions, Dare to Make A Difference - Success 101 for Teens, Spread Some Love - Relationships 101 (Workbook) and Quotes Unlimited.

After those publications in 2009, Andrews recorded his hit novel as well as Whose Woman Was She? and When the Dust Settles - I am Still Standing: his True Hollywood Story, now also being turned into a film.

New titles in the Personal Development genre include: Quotes Unlimited Vol. II, The FIVE "Ps" For Teens, Dare to Make A Difference -

Success 101 and Dare to Make A Difference - Success 101 - The Teacher's Guide.

His new translated titles include: Chico Rudo ... El Imparable, Cuya Mujer Fue Ella? and Rude Buay ... The Unstoppable in Chinese.

Back in 2009, while writing the introduction of his debut book for teens: Dare To Make A Difference - Success 101 for Teens, Andrews visited the local bookstore. He discovered only 5 books in the Personal Development genre for teens while noticing hundreds of the same genre in the adult section. Sensing there was a lack of personal growth resources, focusing on youth 13-21, he published his teen book and soon thereafter founded Teen Success.

This organization is empowerment based, designed to empower Teens in maximizing their full potential to be successful and contributing citizens in the world.

Andrews, referred to as the man with "the golden voice" is a sought after speaker on "Success" targeting young adults. He recently addressed teens in New York, Los Angeles, Hawaii and was the guest speaker at the 2011 Dr. Martin Luther King Jr. birthday celebrations in Eugene, Oregon.

John Andrews is from a home of educators; all five of his sisters taught school - two acquiring the status of school principals. Though self - educated, he understands the benefits of a great education and being all he can be. Two of his teenage sons are also writers. John spends most of his time writing, publishing books and traveling the country going on book tours.

Additionally, John Andrews is a screenwriter and producer, and is in (2012) turning his bestselling novel into a film.

See more about the author in his memoir:
Two books in one volume.
HOW I RAISED MYSELF FROM FAILURE
TO SUCCESS IN HOLLYWOOD.

"I firmly believe that any man's finest hour, the greatest fulfillment of all that he holds dear, is the moment when he has worked his heart out in a good cause and lies exhausted on the field of battle - victorious"

- VINCE LOMBARDI

http://thinkexist.com/quotation/i_firmly_believe_that_any_man-s_finest_hour-the/173395.html

FOR MORE ON
BOOKS THAT WILL ENHANCE YOUR LIFE ™
Visit: **A L I**
www.AndrewsLeadershipInternational.com
EMAIL US
presales@therudebuay.com

Website
www.theRUDEBUAY.com

*Rude Buay is a drug prevention chronicle about teens caught up in the war on drugs and contains content for adults; parental discretion is advised for children.

A NEW RELEASE

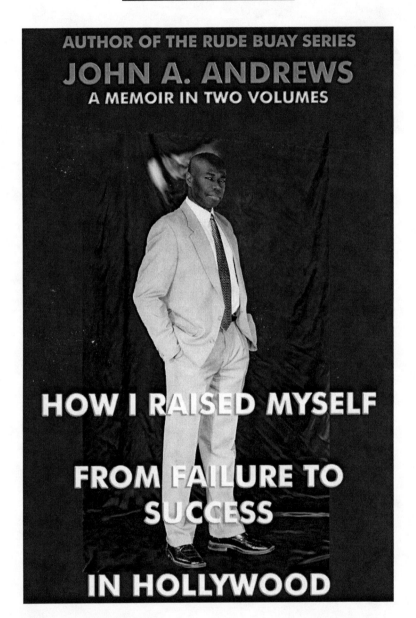

AUTHOR OF THE RUDE BUAY SERIES

JOHN A. ANDREWS

A MEMOIR IN TWO VOLUMES

HOW I RAISED MYSELF

FROM FAILURE TO SUCCESS

IN HOLLYWOOD

<u>OTHER RELEASES</u>

How I Wrote 8 Books In One Year

JOHN A.
ANDREWS

A

Author of
TOTAL COMMITMENT
The Mindset Of Champions

RUDE BUAY ... THE UNSTOPPABLE

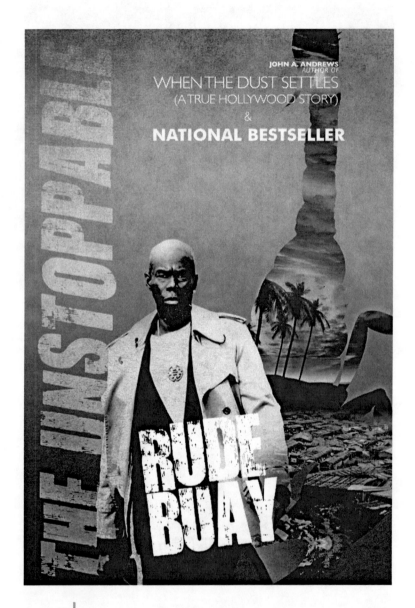

QUOTES UNLIMITED II

ANDREWS

"QUOTES"

UNLIMITED

Vol. II

Over 400 Quotes From Over 18 Books!

John A. Andrews

National Bestselling Author of

RUDE BUAY ... THE UNSTOPPABLE

DARE TO MAKE A DIFFERENCE – SUCCESS 101

National Bestselling Author

Dare To Make A Difference

SUCCESS 101

JOHN A. ANDREWS

TOTAL COMMITMENT

WHEN THE DUST SETTLES

WHOSE WOMAN WAS SHE?

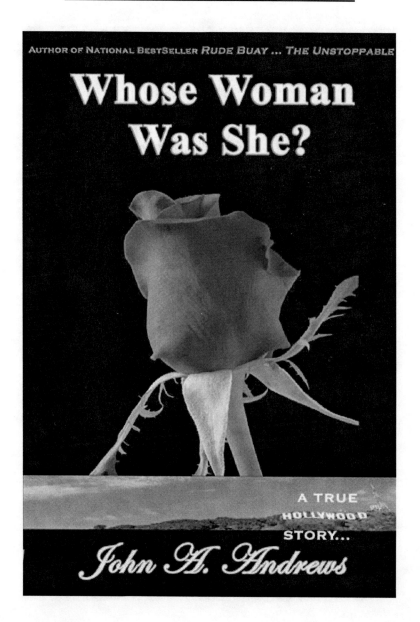

CHICO RUDO ... EL IMPARABLE

**RUDE BUAY ... THE UNSTOPPABLE
CHINESE EDITION**

COMING SOON

CHICO RUDO ... El INTOCABLE

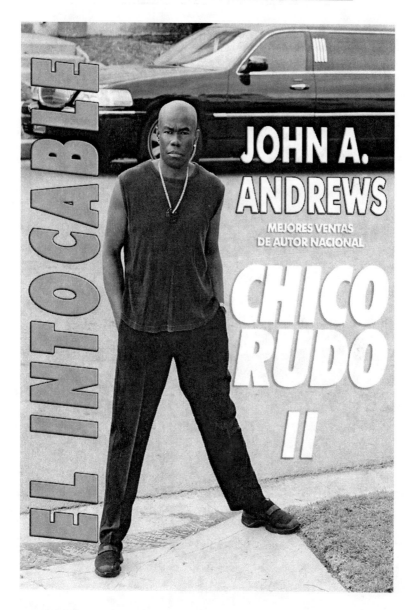

CROSS ATLANTIC FIASCO

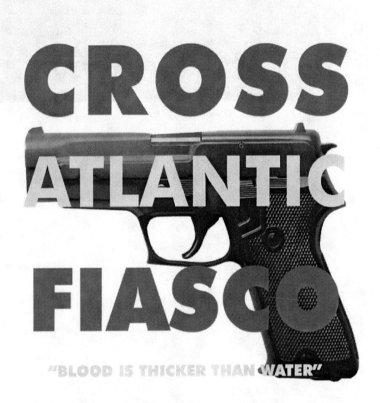

CROSS ATLANTIC FIASCO

"BLOOD IS THICKER THAN WATER"

JOHN A. ANDREWS

National Bestselling Author

of

RUDE BUAY ... THE UNSTOPPABLE

WHO SHOT THE SHERRIFF?

John A. Andrews

WHO

SHOT

THE

SHERRIFF?

National Bestselling Author of

RUDE BUAY ... THE UNSTOPPABLE

RUDE BUAY ... SHATTERPROOF

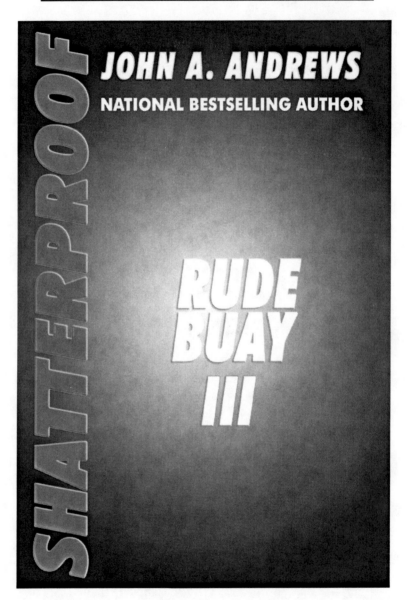

001 ... ONE MAN STANDING

JOHN A. ANDREWS
Author of
The Rude Buay Series

001

One Man Standing

~ A Novel ~

VISIT: WWW.BOOKSTHATWILLENHANCEYOURLIFE.COM

CPSIA information can be obtained at www.ICGtesting.com
Printed in the USA
LVOW041515270312

275001LV00002B/48/P